P9-BTY-567

WHISPERS FROM THE PAST

MAXINE BOLT

AVALON BOOKS
THOMAS BOUREGY AND COMPANY, INC.
401 LAFAYETTE STREET
NEW YORK, NEW YORK 10003

Library of Congress Card Number: 90-90341
ISBN 0-8034-8837-8

PRINTED IN THE UNITED STATES OF AMERICA
BY HADDON CRAFTSMEN, SCRANTON, PENNSYLVANIA

To Patricia Penix Manthey, Herbert Manthey,
Susie and John Harris, and Linda and Curtis Penix, Jr.

Chapter One

Andrea Maxwell parked her car beside the antiquated garage that sat the width of the lawn away from the farmhouse. It was a windy day at the witching end of October, and she got out into the sharp, cold air that had blown up off the sea, bringing with it the distinctive smell of the salt marshes. The sudden gust gathered a scattering of red-gold leaves, already past their peak of color, tinged brown at the edges. They swirled across the lawn like confetti, coming to rest against the bank of colorful chrysanthemums that framed the house.

Lost in the puzzling memory of an earlier incident, Andrea reached up absentmindedly to brush at a leaf that had caught in her hair. Anyone observing might have mistaken her for an autumn sprite. Her shoulder-length, red-gold hair, full and silky, was lifted by the wind and swirled in tendrils across her face.

Her eyes, thoughtful and large, were the pale brown of late-autumn leaves.

She drew her russet-colored coat closer against the chill and headed for the kitchen entrance to the house. She hoped Carla Hopkins would be home. This first day of her assignment to write a series on Atlantic County, New Jersey, had been disturbing, and she needed someone to talk to.

As she came inside, the kitchen was warm and welcoming. There was the fresh-cider smell of autumn apples, and a kettle on the stove hummed merrily. Carla, taking something from the oven, turned to smile at her. "I timed that just right, didn't I? I said to myself, 'That young woman will be coming back in early evening, and I'll bet a hot pot of coffee and some warm cinnamon rolls will be just what the doctor ordered.' "

Andrea resisted the urge to hug the kind older woman. She had known her less than two days, but she was already developing a genuine affection for her. "Oh, Carla, I'm so glad Randolph arranged for me to stay with you," she said. "I'd have hated it if he'd put me up in one of those crowded hotels in Atlantic City."

"I want you to stay with Carla Hopkins while you're on this assignment," her editor, Randolph Kenyon, had told her. "It will save money—which we need to do until we get this venture out of the red—and you'll get the flavor of the area you're writing about much better because you'll be right in the middle of it. Carla is my mother's cousin. You'll like her." As usual, Randolph was right. She had liked Carla immediately.

"I'm glad he thought of it too," Carla said, bringing the coffeepot to the kitchen table and motioning Andrea to sit across from her. "It seems an eternity since there has been a young person living here."

"These are heavenly." Andrea closed her eyes as she took the first bite of the roll Carla placed in front of her.

"I won't pretend I made them." A smile lifted the corners of Carla's mouth. "They came from a bakery in Somers Point. My only contribution was to put them in a warm oven."

Andrea grinned back at her hostess. She never would have mistaken Carla for a farm woman. There was something of the elegance of an actress about her. Her thick, dark hair, with its wide streak of gray beginning at the temples, was pulled back into a chignon that was more chic than severe. Her dark indigo eyes glinted intelligence as well as kindness and humor. But it was her dress that removed her from any true association with farming: Her skirt was made of floor-length burgundy velvet and was worn over a black body suit.

"Randolph told me that you moved out here to the shore only recently. He also said that you're from Philadelphia, and you were—are—an artist," Andrea said.

"I taught art. There's a difference. I lacked something—touch, vision, whatever. . . . But I like to think that the thirty years I spent as an art teacher in the public schools weren't wasted, either. A handful of my students went on to achieve what I couldn't."

"And you moved out here after you retired?"

"Yes, two years ago." A shadow of sadness touched her face briefly. "Benton, my husband, lived only one year after our early retirement. We had so much looked forward to this. . . ."

Andrea reached across the table to touch her hand. "I'm sorry. Randolph told me you have two children. Do they live near?"

Carla shook her head. "Benton, Jr., is in Japan. He's been with a company there for years, and Lisa lives in California. This farmhouse had been in Benton's family for three generations, however, so even though I'm alone, I'd rather stay here than sell it and move back to Philadelphia. More coffee?" she asked, as if to change the subject to more pleasant matters.

"Yes, please." Andrea pushed her cup slightly forward, glancing around the kitchen. The farmhouse had obviously recently undergone renovation, and Carla had apparently used some of her denied artistic talent to keep intact a modern yet warm feeling in this country kitchen.

From the entrance door, three steps led up to the room. On the left, a big white range was tucked in a corner alcove. To the right of the entrance, a counter ran the length of the wall. The cabinets were a warm, yellow wood, and the door fronts were of a darker caning. A whole rack of pots, pans, spoons, cups, and kettles decorated the pale ecru wall above the round kitchen table in the window alcove. Andrea noticed a collage of cut-out photos of children along one wall.

Carla, following her gaze, smiled. "My grandchildren. I have six of them, seldom seen, so I keep their pictures there in a kind of human time line, updating as they grow."

"Clever. That ceramic gingerbread house above the cabinet—did you make it?"

"No. The ceramic side of art was never quite my thing. I saw it in a mail-order catalog and couldn't resist it—the only things here that I did are those skillets over there by the stove. Took some old useless ones, enameled them blue, and painted the geese on them."

"They go so well with the goose canister set." Andrea nodded to where a row of white geese in graduated sizes marched across the back of the counter, holding their supplies of flour, coffee, sugar, and tea.

"Now tell me about your day. Did you get any good leads to start writing your series?" Carla asked.

Andrea paused, holding her coffee cup in both hands. She looked out the window to where, in the paling evening sunlight, the leaves continued to fall, blowing like small, lost things set adrift in the wind. She shivered slightly, feeling again the chill of something mysterious that had tinged her day. "I didn't get much—not what I'd hoped, anyway. It was more as if I'd come upon something secret . . . and sinister."

Carla raised quizzical eyebrows. "Sinister? Whatever do you mean? I thought you were doing a nature series about the lesser-known areas of Atlantic County, the pine woods and the hidden-away villages."

"That was . . . is the assignment. But I seem to have opened up another story—a murder that was never solved."

The surprised look on Carla's face remained as she waited for her to continue.

"The thing is," Andrea went on, not sure how to explain the feeling that was based more on instinct than fact, "a lot of people mistook me for someone else."

Carla laughed with relief. "That's not so unusual. It happens to all of us at one time or another, I think. . . ."

"But it wasn't as simple as that. You see, the girl I was mistaken to be is dead. And I got the feeling that some of the people who saw me weren't happy at all that she has a lookalike. Some of them were downright hostile, or just plain scared."

Carla laughed again. This time there was more gaiety in the sound. "I think it's the time of year."

"Excuse me?"

"It's close to Halloween. I expect you ran into some of the old-timers around these parts who still attribute—especially in this season—anything they can't explain to being the work of the Jersey Devil."

"The Jersey Devil?" Andrea echoed, astonished.

"Yes, a bit of folklore. A large chunk, actually, where this area is concerned, since this is the country where he was born."

"What exactly *is* the Jersey Devil?" Andrea asked, still mystified.

"It's an old legend that still circulates

in the pine barrens and rural areas of South Jersey. You'd be surprised how many people believe that any mischief that occurs around the time of Halloween is an act of the devil. I actually had one neighbor out this way tell me in all seriousness that this demon had visited her house in the night and caused a cake she had baked to grow hair!" Carla shook her head in amusement. "Apparently it never occurred to her that it was plain old mold growing on the cake; scientific fact, not the unseen."

"But what started such an idea? What is this story of this Jersey Devil based on?"

"As I recall, it dates back to the early settlers. There was a woman named Leeds, and like the Old Woman in the Shoe, she had entirely too many children. When she found there was to be yet another, she put a curse on the unborn child and said she hoped it would belong to the devil. In late October, when the child was born, so the story goes, it was like no baby anyone had seen ever before. A creature with cloven hooves and horns, it took wing and flew out the window. As legend tells it, the demon has been wandering the woods of South Jersey ever since. You will find people who, in all seriousness, tell you they have glimpsed him on dark nights, flying about on his errands of evil."

"Incredible!" Andrea laughed, not quite able to believe that people anywhere let their superstitions go to such lengths. Yet her mind was already moving ahead to the story she would write and how she might incorporate this legend into it.

"I invited a few people over tonight," Carla said, getting up from the table. "Randolph asked me to make sure you met a 'composite representation' of the natives while you're here. How long has he been publishing—what's the name of the magazine?"

"*Kaleidoscope.* It's a kind of experimental publication, not quite a newspaper, not quite a magazine, either. I think 'glossy tabloid' would be the best way to describe it. It's published twice a month, and attempts an overview of the Pennsylvania, New Jersey, Delaware, and Maryland area. He's hoping for some of the appeal of a supermarket tabloid, but he's aiming at a more literary reader too. Actually, this is only the sixth issue coming out, so it's quite new."

"And you've been with him since the beginning?"

"Yes. I came on at the start. I've known Randolph from when we both worked on a city daily. He was an investigative reporter there, and I was a reporter with no specific assignment. He offered me a column with my own byline, and that was reason enough to go with him."

"I'm sure that must mean you're very good at what you do. I know I wouldn't want to start a new publication without the best talent I could find."

Andrea smiled modestly. "I don't think it hurts that his wife, Jeannie, and I were college friends. We were roommates the last two years at Bryn Mawr. I got in on the ground floor with Randolph that way, I suppose. Otherwise, he might never have noticed the stories I wrote."

"I'm sure talent played a large part too," Carla assured her. "Now, speaking of friends, I'm sure you'll find some compatible young people in this group I've invited tonight. When I let it be known that our guest of honor was a pretty reporter from the city, it was no problem at all for my friends to persuade their young relatives to put in an appearance."

Andrea smiled. "Thanks, Carla. I hoped there was another way to meet people here other than today's experience."

"You probably met up with only a few of the more superstitious folks. Tonight should get you off to a good start, gathering the kind of material you need." She glanced at the blue ceramic clock above the entrance door. "We'll have dinner at seven. Nothing elaborate, just spaghetti, salad, and garlic bread. You've time to freshen your makeup, change, or whatever. . . ."

"Is there anything I can do to help in the kitchen?"

"No. Domesticity not being my forte, I've asked Lydia Markum, my cleaning woman, to do the cooking. It's all taken care of."

In her comfortable room, Andrea sat at the dressing table, leaning in close to the mirror as if she expected her reflected image to yield some secret knowledge.

Who was this girl, three years dead and gone, to whom she bore such a strong resemblance? The startled reactions had all come from people who inhabited the same place, a wild, rustic section of the county where a network of narrow little sandy trails snaked through the pine trees.

While driving through she had stopped at a small country store to buy a candy bar, also hoping that she might collect some interesting background information from the owner. Instead, she had opened the door to horrified disbelief. "It's Cheryl!" someone had screamed. "Cheryl Kendexter!"

In the confusion that followed, all Andrea had learned was that Cheryl Kendexter had been found murdered three years ago, and no one had ever solved the crime. As for her own explanations as to who she was and why she was there, she was met with more suspicion than belief. She had left shortly after, knowing her presence was not a welcome one.

That the place was in one of the poorer sections of the county was obvious. Poverty had left its depressing mark, evidenced by scattered shacks with peeling paint and cluttered, junk-filled yards. Andrea had always had the strange sensation that she understood poverty, the sight, the feel, the smell of it, better than there was any reason for her to do so. As an only child, born to parents already approaching middle age and comfortably well-to-do, there had been no grounds for this fancy.

Sometimes, and then so briefly that it was gone before she could put it into focus, she had the odd sensation of a life lived before in another place—an episode gone out of reliable memory, but one that left an unsettling feeling. She vaguely remembered an old decaying house with a leaking roof and broken windowpanes. She shook her head. *Watch it,* she told herself. *You're going to become as superstitious as those people who believe in the Jersey Devil. . . .*

She turned her attention to the impending party. What should she wear? She decided to check with Carla. Walking out of her room, she heard her hostess's voice coming from the kitchen. She hurried in that direction just in time to see that Carla was admitting a large, blond woman into the room. The newcomer, glancing over Carla's shoulder and seeing Andrea, stopped short. Her face went deadly white. "Cheryl." It was a horrified whisper. She placed her hand over her heart. "Oh, the saints keep and preserve us!"

Chapter Two

Before Andrea was dressed, she heard the first of the guests begin to arrive. Taking her cue from Carla's rather elegant attire, she took a scoop-neck black dress from her closet, added gold chains and her best high-heel black sandals. She hoped these people would prove to be less superstitious than those she had dealt with earlier. She was still shaken by Lydia Markum's extreme reaction.

It had actually taken some persuasive power on the part of Carla to induce Lydia to calm down, or even to remain and prepare the meal. "But she's the very image of Cheryl—the spitting image. I tell you, it's the work of the devil himself!" Lydia kept repeating.

Carla, giving Andrea a wry look, had seated Lydia at the kitchen table with a cup of coffee. "It's rather unkind of you to use such terms in regard to Andrea. She's so completely new to this place, I had to draw a map for her this morning just so she could find her way around. Anyway, haven't you heard the old saw about how each of us has a lookalike somewhere? Come on, now! What will she write about us in her column if we act this way?"

In the end, Lydia had apologized. "It's just that you took me so by surprise at first," she said. But even then, Andrea had heard her mutter something about a doppelgänger under her breath.

"Who was Cheryl Kendexter?" Andrea asked when she felt it was safe to discuss the subject with Lydia.

"She was my next-door neighbor's daughter," Lydia answered. "She was killed three years ago at Halloween. They found her body in the gravel pit out on Point Road."

"And there was no clue at all as to who killed her?"

"No. None. It seemed like it was hushed up on purpose."

"Why would that be?" Andrea asked.

Lydia gave her a long, searching look. "Who's to say? For my part, I always thought it was a little too close to the law for the law to look into it." With that, as if she knew she had said too much, she pressed her mouth shut in a tight, prim line and got up to busy herself with the meal. Try as she might, Andrea was unable to draw her out again on the subject.

Now dressed, Andrea shook her head at her reflection in the mirror and began massaging her face with her fingers, slowly and deliberately, as if to change her features before she went out to meet the guests.

The group certainly was a composite, she thought as Carla began to introduce her to the assemblage in the living room. It might well have been a costume party. The first was a giant of a man in torn jeans and an Irish fisherman's sweater. He dominated the room as much by personality as size. *A Viking,* Andrea thought as he came toward her smiling, hand outstretched. She could visualize him sailing in from distant shores, a Norse god come to claim a new land.

"Ian Gershner," Carla said. Now, looking up into his face, Andrea realized who he was. Ian Gershner's mystic paintings of the sea were prominently displayed in office buildings and art galleries in the Philadelphia area. She hadn't recognized him in this attire, his reddish hair and beard untrimmed. His photographs had always shown him in coat and tie, impeccably groomed. She was awed by his easy familiarity in Carla's house.

"Suppose I build a fire in the library," he suggested. "It might be more cozy if we eat in there instead of your dining room. We could put those two long tables together and set them for dinner. . . ."

"Good idea," Carla agreed, giving his arm an affectionate pat. Then she steered Andrea toward an older couple whom she had noticed earlier arriving in a pickup truck. "Warren and Bertha Putnam. They're neighbors from a nearby farm." Bertha might have been the model for *American Gothic.* Her pale hair was pulled back in a tight wisp of a bun, and the checkered gingham dress she wore gave her a 1930s look. Warren was heavyset, and the muscles that bulged against the sleeves of his blue shirt and his tan cotton work pants indicated a lifetime spent hefting big loads. Although, unlike Lydia, they tried to conceal their astonishment, Andrea knew from the way they looked at her that they, too, had marked her resemblance to Cheryl.

Andrea was most drawn to the next guest to whom she was introduced, and she thought with some amusement that this was an attempt at matchmaking on Carla's part. Carla made a pretense of being too casual in bringing them together, but at the same time, she gave each more than a casual biography of the other.

Byron Standish, Andrea learned, was a lawyer, an assistant in the district attorney's office. *A guy on his way up,* she thought as she greeted him. *And handsome at that.* His gray eyes had a probing, yet not unfriendly gaze. Unlike the guests she'd been introduced to so far, he was nattily dressed in a dark suit, white shirt, and a maroon, figured tie. Yet, politeness aside, he didn't give the impression that he was especially happy to be here. Andrea wondered if his presence had required some measure of arm-twisting.

Nevertheless, he stayed at her side, acting as a gallant but unofficial escort. "You ought to get some story out of this assortment," he said, grinning down at her. "Criminals, suspects, farmers, social butterflies—Carla has managed to get them all under one roof."

Andrea looked closely at the next man to be introduced, Frank Heiler. She had the vague feeling that he had been present in the country store where her entrance had caused such pandemonium. If he had been, he betrayed no recognition. She guessed Frank was about her own age—twenty-five. He wore his leather jacket and jeans with a casual slouch. His full-lipped mouth seemed poised to pout or sneer. In a somewhat seedy way, he was good-looking, with dark-blond hair, overly long and curling, blue eyes, and sharply drawn features in a thin face. She noted with surprise that he and Byron appeared to be well acquainted.

The most conspicuous, and also the most attractive, in a flashy sort of way, was a young couple who looked to be in their late teens or early twenties. The woman, apparently misunderstanding the informality of the gathering, wore a strapless emerald dress with a sequined bodice. The points of the jagged hemline barely touched her knees. A heavy glitter of fake diamonds adorned her neck, ears, and wrists.

She was introduced as Jade Stone, but Andrea was sure the name had about as much authenticity as her jewelry, even before Frank said, "She's plain old Emma Jane Johnson out here in the woods—Jade Stone in the Atlantic City nightclubs where she works as a dancer."

"Plain I never was, and you, Frank Heiler, of all people, should remember that!" Her toss of long platinum hair was followed by an insinuating look at Frank. Ignoring it, he only grinned and gave Andrea a conspiratorial wink.

"Fancied herself a Jade since grade school, because of her eyes," he said. It was true: Her eyes, though cold, were exceptionally green.

Jade's companion, looking bored with the whole exchange, barely acknowledged his introduction. "Tony Bandelli," Byron said briefly, taking her arm almost at once and turning her toward other guests. Fascinated, Andrea still glanced over her shoulder at them. Tony was also dressed in evening clothes. Short but slim, he had the good looks of a movie idol, and she guessed his self-admiration to be equal to Jade's.

Rounding out the guests were a family whose patrician good looks and quiet, expensive clothes branded them as the socialites Byron had mentioned earlier. "Ellen and Simon Bentley and their daughter Antonia," Carla said. "The Bentleys live in that big Georgian house you admired out near The Point."

Simon and Ellen acknowledged her with pleasant, correct nods. Antonia looked at her briefly and held out her hand.

"I've been following *Kaleidoscope* and have read all your columns," Ellen told her. "When I heard at the club the other day that you were to do a series about our little world out here at the shore, I insisted that Carla invite us. I have some stories I know you can use."

Andrea thanked her before she moved away. She found this in all her assignments, people who wanted for one reason or another to get their own pet projects into print. Yet she was a little surprised. The Bentleys were the sort she would expect to avoid, rather than seek, publicity. The daughter, Antonia, although still attractive, had the pinched, tired look of a woman past her prime who had seen life slip by, and who was a little stunned that nothing of any real interest had come of it.

"Old maid," Frank whispered when they were out of earshot.

Ian came into the room to announce that he had a blazing fire going in the library and that Lydia was about ready to serve. It was Andrea's first look inside this room at the front of the house. Like the kitchen, it showed signs of recent renovation. Apparently a partition wall had been removed to incorporate two former rooms into this one. The dark ceiling beams, the sea-gray paneling, and even the big stone fireplace were all obviously new.

It took a stretch of the imagination to call this room a library. There were two narrow bookcases on either side of the fireplace, each only partially filled. This long room had been made to order for entertaining. Andrea thought with a touch of sadness that Carla's husband had never enjoyed it with her.

The two tables were covered with an ivory cloth and the centerpiece had been done with Halloween in mind. An enormous blue granite bowl held an assortment of chrysanthemums, autumn foliage, and above this, mounted on a thin rod so transparent as to make him appear to be in flight, was a papier-mâché Jersey Devil. A grinning figure of malevolence and mystery, he appeared almost as an intentional omen.

Andrea was pleased to find she was seated next to Byron. Glancing across the table, she was a little bemused to see Antonia paired with Frank. A more unlikely twosome would be hard to find.

"Lydia, where is your plate?" Carla asked, nodding toward the vacant chair and empty space at the table. "You were invited to eat with us, you know, not just prepare the meal."

"I moved it to the kitchen," Lydia said, lips compressed. "There are twelve people seated at this table and I'm not going to be the thirteenth."

"Oh, now Lydia—" Carla began, only to be interrupted.

"It's enough bad luck to bring that graven image of the devil himself to the table. I tell you, it's flying in the face of providence. Something bad will come of it, you'll see!"

Carla shook her head as she watched her hurry away. "I thought in making this centerpiece, I was paying tribute to local lore, not bringing on bad luck."

"I will never understand," Ellen remarked, "why it is that all these otherwise sensible people around here are so bent on perpetuating this myth of the Jersey Devil."

Her husband had apparently tapped her foot under the table. She started quickly, stared at him, and then flushed slightly, adding, "I meant the natives, of course, Carla. In bringing the Jersey Devil to the table, you were only acknowledging our legend."

Carla accepted Ellen's faux pas with a humorous shrug. "I'm sure the myth of the devil will be useful to Andrea in writing about South Jersey. I know all of you can contribute stories for the series she plans to do."

"I should think, coming from Philadelphia, you're already pretty familiar with the Jersey Shore," Simon said.

"Actually, no. Sometimes it seemed to me that we were the only people in Philadelphia who never spent a single summer weekend out here."

"Remarkable. The beaches become so crowded in summer, I sometimes wonder if all Philadelphia hasn't moved out here en masse. Where did you spend your holidays?" His keen gray eyes were fixed on her as if it might be important to know.

"My family had a cabin in the Poconos. We seldom missed a weekend going there."

"In that case, I suppose you'll want to start from scratch learning about Atlantic City and the surrounding country."

Andrea nodded. It did seem odd, now it had come up, that considering the proximity to the city she and her family had never visited this seashore resort. The Pocono habit had been established early, however, and her mother had professed an aversion to the seashore. "It's hot, the sand is a misery, and the salt water does awful things to your hair," she had protested when Andrea had wanted to come here with school friends. "You'd hate it. Ask your friends to come to the mountains with us instead."

A sudden nostalgia came over her for

those days gone by—the house in Society Hill, the holidays spent away, the inevitable preparations before each weekend. The house had been sold by her attorney guardian after her parents' death. The plane crash had been devastating in its finality. It was the income from the sale that financed her education and now supplemented her salary, allowing her the small apartment near the art museum and Fairmont Park. She had managed to hang onto the cabin in the Poconos. Sometimes it seemed that it was all that remained of her childhood.

Lydia, her superstitions aside, had prepared and served an excellent meal, and the guests, in spite of their dissimilarity, had proved talkative and cheerful. They chattered among each other about recent events, the politics of the community, and the latest gossip about their assorted friends. They gave Andrea frequent explanations.

By the time Lydia brought dessert, a rich German chocolate cake served in giant wedges with mugs of fresh coffee, the gathering had left the table to group around the fire, seated on sofas and armchairs. Ian added logs when the flames diminished. Andrea, listening to the stories, wished she had brought pen and notebook.

Warren and Bertha proved more articulate than their initial appearance had led her to believe. Warren spoke knowledgeably about agriculture. "New Jersey is called the 'Garden State' because of the large amount of produce grown here," he explained. "Much of it is raised on small farms, or 'garden patches.' "

"But there are numerous large farms as well," Bertha added, "mostly commercial growers with huge operations that require large numbers of migrant workers."

"And we've always had good soil, climate, and ready supplies of water to make it conducive to crop growing," Warren said.

"It's one of the oldest settlements in the United States, isn't it?" Andrea inquired.

"It is, indeed," Simon told her. "Before the middle of the 1600s there were already established colonies of Dutch and Swedish settlers."

"Of course, before these colonists," Bertha said, "the land was the territory of the Leni-Lenape Indians. In fact, the early name for what we call New Jersey was 'Sheichbi.' In the Leni-Lenape Indian language, that means 'land along the water.' "

"It may have been a resort even before the European settlers came," Ian said. "The casinos are fairly recent, but Atlantic City goes back a long way."

"But remember how deserted the streets used to be in winter before the casinos moved in?" Ellen asked.

"Yes," Ian said. "I recall when one could drive the whole length of the island and see almost no one in winter, but in the summertime, it could take forever to negotiate one block."

Interspersed with her fact gathering, Andrea was also becoming acquainted with Byron. He had relocated to this area only a year ago and had never heard of Cheryl. When she explained a little of that mystery to him, he offered to do some research and get back to her. Andrea realized, as she looked into his mesmerizing gray eyes, that she was looking forward to seeing him again.

When the last log on the fire had burned to embers, the guests began to collect their coats to leave. Andrea, standing in front of the dying fire, was thanking them for the time they had given to get her column started. She was standing in an unconscious but characteristic pose, right hip thrust out, left heel against her right instep, her coffee cup lifted as she spoke. It was then she became aware of how all the guests were watching her, a hushed, haunted expression on their faces. She knew instinctively they were thinking of Cheryl, the one subject they had avoided discussing.

It was Jade Stone, made bold by bad manners, who stepped forward, raking her up and down with her hard green eyes. "We all know you aren't interested in writing a series about the Jersey Shore," she said. "You came to stir up that old murder. Who was Cheryl Kendexter to you?"

Chapter Three

The house Andrea was wandering through might well have been a figment of Ian Gershner's imaginative paint-brush. The colors were the blues and grays of a stormy sea; the images muted as if viewed through a mist. The wind cried softly through the empty rooms and a spattering of rain fell like tears on the roof.

It was an old sea captain's house, where some weight of the past nagged at her half-memories of another lifetime. Although Andrea was inside, she could see the exterior: the widow's walk facing the open waters of the Atlantic, the rotted railings, broken and falling away.

The house was beyond redemption now. All the former inhabitants were dead and gone, yet something lingered—holographic images suspended in vacant rooms. Sound also moved through the echoing space—the washing sigh of waves on the shore, voices calling, urgent and angry, in some far room.

Someone was there. Someone waited behind a broken door. The ineffable communication of some living presence overwhelmed her, drew her deeper into the house. She searched, running through the maze of corridors and unlocked rooms, coming finally against a wall—a wall that had no door. Yet, behind it, she knew, lurked the unknown entity.

Andrea ran back to the front of the house to find the mist had parted. The moon, a round blood-red globe, hung close and ominous, dripping its color in mirrorlike spatters across the water. And there, atop the moon, riding it as if it were a bucking bronco, sat the Jersey Devil. Malevolent and evil, his demon eyes stared directly into her own.

She sat up quickly, mouth formed into a scream, already reaching out for some object to throw at the apparition, but the grinning devil was gone and she found she was bolt upright in bed, holding a small figurine from the nightstand in a tightly closed fist. It was some seconds before she realized she was coming out of a nightmare. Beside her, the lighted numerals of the clock indicated it was ten minutes after four.

She switched on the lamp, but the warm glow only partially restored reality. Some part of her spirit was still stranded in the landscape of the dream. It had been almost midnight when the last of the guests had departed, and although she had slept a scant four hours, she knew she would sleep no more tonight.

The dream had been especially disturbing because she was not at all prone to nightmares, and, in fact, seldom remembered any dream she had. She looked toward the darkened bedroom window that faced the pine woods, almost expecting to see the dream replayed there like moving images on a screen.

The drapery was not drawn across the window, nor had she pulled the shade. The window of the farmhouse faced away from the road, but now, with the light inside and the darkness out, she felt exposed. Hurriedly she got out of bed and pulled the shade against the darkness. At the mirror, she paused, staring as if at a stranger. Who was this girl who had lived in this community, died a violent death, and who, if people were to be believed, had been almost a clone of herself?

She shuddered, wanting to put aside the idea that this had any connection with her, but she had the nagging feeling that it did, that it was more than just a monstrous coincidence.

Still, in the dark hours before dawn it was too easy to let suspicion get the upper hand. A little paranoia was in everyone at this wakeful hour, she knew. Cheryl Kendexter needed to be put into perspective. Hadn't Carla explained how superstition overshadowed the thinking of many of the people who lived here? A belief in the unknown threaded through too much of their conversation.

Somewhere in the pine woods, an eerie voice screamed once and then was silent. A screech owl, she told herself. She had heard them many times, haunting the woodlands of the Poconos. A stretch of the Garden State Parkway ran through the pines behind Carla's house. The swishing sound of traffic moved like a whisper through the trees. She listened to the grinding sound when an occasional truck entered and exited at the

Somers Point ramp. Normal sounds, she told herself. City sounds interspersed with the noises of the woods. Nothing of the occult here.

The best way to deal with her wakefulness would be to start writing the first of her columns. She removed the cover from her portable word processor and went to work.

Atlantic County, New Jersey, is a land of contrasts. The rich and famous, high rollers, and ordinary tourists haunt the casinos of Atlantic City, while the Jersey Devil haunts the pines of its rural regions. The pine barrens of Burlington County reach out into these wild, rustic areas on one side, and the sea reaches its tentacles in on the other.

Encouraged by her opening paragraph, Andrea continued to write the article, rereading frequently and making changes. When she was almost finished, she paused, thought briefly, and added:

The pines hold secrets. The sea wind whispers through the trees and the people whisper to each other about the death of Cheryl Kendexter, a young woman murdered so close to Halloween that the superstitious say it was the work of the Jersey Devil. Others say the crime was too close to the power structure to allow solution. Only a few—possibly only one person—know the truth.

"Andrea?" She jumped, startled at the sound of Carla's firm rap on the door. "Are you awake? It's almost eight o'clock."

"Already? Where does time go?" She switched off the word processor and opened the door.

Carla was dressed for the day. Her hair was coiled on top of her head and she was wearing a navy-blue sweater over gray flannel slacks. Her face, still flawlessly smooth, bore the trace of blusher and lipstick. Her eyes, outlined with dark mascara, were large and clear. Andrea smiled at her in admiration. Carla, she sensed, would never be an old woman at any age.

"You said you wanted to get up early

despite the late hour you went to bed. There's coffee ready in the kitchen."

"I've been up since four o'clock. Bad dream," Andrea explained, making a wry face. "I knew I wouldn't sleep again, so I worked on the column. I had no idea it was so late! Time does get away when I'm writing."

"I know all about that! It gets away from me when I'm painting." She paused, looking at Andrea keenly. "Bad dream? Did you hear too much talk of the Jersey Devil, or that unfortunate Cheryl last night?"

"A little, probably. I dreamed of a frightening place, and the Jersey Devil was in it. It all seemed too real."

Carla continued to watch her curiously, seemed about to say something, then turned away abruptly. "Come to the kitchen when you're ready. What you need is a good breakfast."

Andrea lifted the shade. Sunshine came through the trees and slid inside the window, leaving patches of light on the bedroom floor. It was going to be a lovely day. With the memory of the dream fading, she felt her spirits lift in a quick thrill of anticipation. Byron

Standish—his name and image floated through her mind. She wasn't sure whether it was because of his obligatory reaction to Carla's matchmaking, or if it was because he wanted to, but he had asked her out to dinner tonight. She intended to enjoy herself and forget this pursuit of shadows, the gathering of material, or even writing the series.

The smell of breakfast drifted into the bedroom, giving her an enormous appetite. She pulled a robe over her pajamas and hurried off in the direction of the kitchen.

Carla turned to smile at her. "We have an invitation to lunch today. Ian asked me to bring you to his place. I forgot to mention it to you last night." She paused. "It's not a command performance, you know. If you have other plans, Ian will understand."

"Oh, but I don't! I'd love to go. I really liked Ian."

"Good. I told him you'd want to come when I accepted for you. It'll give you a chance to see some more of the area. Ian lives in Ocean City, down at the very tip of the island."

"I hope I'll see some of his work too.

His sea paintings are the sort of thing Randolph would love to feature in *Kaleidoscope.* Of course, Ian has been profiled so many times, he may not want to do another interview."

"Of course he will. You'll find him more than cooperative. I not only envy his talent, I envy his culinary ability too."

"If yours is as good as it looks, you could give him a run for his money," Andrea said, watching Carla turn an omelet onto her plate.

"Accidental. Purely accidental. I hate to cook. I hate anything domestic, unless it's interior decorating. That I could do, and redo, forever. I missed my calling and became an art teacher with what little talent I had, when I might have made a great interior decorator!"

Andrea noted with a twinge of sympathy that there was something of a lost soul about Carla. Her career was over, her husband dead, her children scattered across the globe, and here she was alone in an old farmhouse—waiting for what? It wasn't fair. There should be something more left for her.

* * *

They left well before noon to keep the luncheon date with Ian. "It's a long avenue of stoplights down the island," Carla said, backing her station wagon out of the garage, "and you never can gauge the traffic." She drove along the almost-deserted country road and through Somers Point, then crossed the bridge that led across the Great Egg Harbor Inlet to Ocean City.

As Carla drove over the bridge, Andrea leaned close against the car window, looking out at the sapphire autumn sky and the waters of the inlet that lay calm and flat as a mirror below them. A flock of sea gulls dipped close, chasing one another against the blue void, screaming in raucous protestation.

For the briefest snatch out of time, Andrea had the feeling that she was viewing a scene she had seen before, or might see again. As if on the same wavelength, Carla glanced at her and said, smiling, "Maybe you'll get sand in your shoes."

"Sand in my shoes?" she asked uncertainly, returning Carla's impish smile.

"Yes. There's a saying here that if you come to the shore and get sand in your shoes, you'll stay. Or you'll always come back. A version of the fairy-tale enchanted forest, I guess."

"You know," Andrea said seriously to Carla, "I can't recall ever being here on the shore a single time in all my life, and yet. . . ."

"What?"

"It seems like I have been here before."

Carla laughed. "Don't let Lydia hear you say that. She already half believes you're the returned spirit of—someone else."

When they had driven the length of the island and had come to the very end, where it appeared that nothing lay between them and the endless blue ocean, Carla made a quick swerve to the right. Andrea clutched the dashboard, feeling for a dizzying second that Carla had lost control of the automobile. Carla, noticing, sent an amused glance in her direction. "This doesn't look like more than a patch of dune grass and pines, does it?"

Andrea now saw that they were on a sandy trail, and a small house lay in front of them. The structure was built of weathered wood and glass. As she had guessed, Ian lived very near the sea. A small second story, which looked as though it had been built around a former upper deck, was all glass in the direction that faced the water. She could imagine the big, affable man up there watching the mists roll in, watching the changing but eternal moods of the sea.

Ian was waiting at the door to greet them when Carla parked the car. "Come in, come in," he said heartily as they stepped up to the entrance. He kissed Carla on the cheek and took Andrea's hand in a warm clasp of greeting. Here was someone she could learn to like a lot, she realized, drawn to him even more than last night.

There was about him none of the remote moodiness often associated with someone whose work was, out of necessity, subjective and produced in isolation. "I'm so glad you could come, Andrea," he said, still holding her hand. "Carla wasn't sure you'd have the time to spare."

"I wouldn't have missed it for the world! Thank you for inviting me."

Ian led them into a big front room, sparsely furnished but inviting in warmth. A great curve of sofa, positioned in front of the fireplace, dominated the center of the room. Here, as last night in Carla's library, he had a bright fire burning. The bleached bones of driftwood logs lay piled nearby on the great stone hearth.

The natural gray stone of the fireplace made up most of the width of the room; the other walls were hung like a gallery with Ian's seascapes. She went at once to examine them. Although familiar with his work, she had not seen it in this quantity before. Looking at the paintings now, she could well understand why Ian's work was based more on the ethereal quality of the image portrayed than on pure realism. The paintings displayed here all bore this same impact.

The seascapes were veiled in mist, and in this overlaid haze, one could almost see imaginary shapes, like undulating spirits in restless movement. She recalled that one unkind critic had written of him that he seemed to view the world with a warped vision.

Carla came to stand beside her. "Ian has exactly what I lack," she remarked, reaching out to touch the misty shape of a boat riding a storm-tossed wave. "I can paint almost anything in its photographic image, but I could never capture its essential spirit."

"His work certainly does have something of the supernatural," Andrea responded.

"Time to eat!" She turned to see Ian standing in the doorway rubbing his hands together. "Lunch is waiting, and I might add it's not made of the stuff that waits well."

They ate in the kitchen. There appeared to be no dining room, and this, too, was simply furnished: Bare windows, pine paneling, a butcher block table with unmatched chairs, an electric range, refrigerator, and a simple cabinet above the sink made up the entire room, giving it a Spartan look. But it was shiny clean, and the warm color of the wood was like sunshine.

Lunch was a soufflé, airy as the mists in Ian's paintings, a superb salad, and hot, pungent tea served in enormous yellow mugs.

"Now you can sample firsthand what I meant when I told you Ian's artistic talent isn't all I envy," Carla said.

"Listen to her!" Ian gave Carla an admiring glance. "This bright, wonderful woman would have you believe she doesn't do anything well. She can do any of the things she *wants* to do, and better than just about anybody I know."

"What I am is basically lazy," Carla conceded. "I don't *like* to cook, and don't *like* to clean up clutter. I never did, and now. . . . Well, cooking for only one seems such a waste of time when there are alternative ways of being fed."

"I being a willing one of them."

Andrea looked up in surprise at the implications of this declaration. Carla, lips slightly parted, seemed to be equally surprised. Andrea had not thought of these two as a romantic pair—only as friends. She guessed Ian to be a few years younger than Carla. But the way he was looking at Carla now as he reached across the table to touch her hand made her wonder if she might not be witnessing a proposal, one that surprised Carla as much as it did her.

She turned her attention discreetly toward the window. Outside, there was no lawn, just a wild expanse of dune grass, sand, and wind-twisted scrub pine trees.

Sea gulls dipped and screamed above the beach. Way out on the horizon, so distant as to appear a mirage, a ship was visible, motionless as a photograph.

Without any reason, Andrea thought suddenly of the house in Society Hill, where cobbled and brick streets and old houses, lovingly restored, nestled together in genteel beauty. How short a distance one could cover in miles and be in what seemed another country—another culture. In a way she hadn't expected, the pull of the sea was drawing her. It was almost as if this was where she belonged, mystery or no.

She must be—what had Carla called it earlier?—getting sand in her shoes. The wild beauty of this secluded beach was breathtaking. She would never hate the seashore as her mother had.

Ian, with the voice of the genial host, brought her back to the present. "So tell me, are you getting the material you want to write, or were you sidetracked by that superstitious lot with their talk of the Jersey Devil?"

Smiling, she turned to find that he was staring at her with an inscrutable look, and a frown had creased his forehead. "Well, yes and no."

He laughed. "An evasive answer if I ever heard one."

"People out our way were making too much about Andrea's being a lookalike to that unfortunate girl who was found dead a few years ago," Carla told him.

The frown lines around Ian's intent blue eyes deepened. "Oh, indeed, yes. But then, I can see now in the light of day that the resemblance *is* remarkable. I didn't notice it last night, being busy with your guests. I can see it now. I can see Cheryl."

Carla glanced at him quickly. "I wasn't aware you knew the young woman, Ian. You didn't tell me. . . ."

"It hadn't come up, I suppose. Cheryl was dead before I met you." A pulse beat became visible at his jaw, which was angrily clenching and unclenching.

"Was this girl someone you knew well?" Carla asked.

"I knew her, but not well. Not nearly as well as I would have wanted." This last was almost a whisper, as if he had forgotten Carla and Andrea and was speaking to himself.

Ever aware of the story that lurked behind the facade, Andrea would have liked to probe, but she was a guest. She watched Ian curiously as he began, somewhat absently, to clear the table. Carla also began to help carry dishes to the sink.

"I'm not as adverse to washing dishes as I am to cooking," she said. "I'll do these now."

"I'll dry." Ian smiled down at her. He was again the genial host.

As the other two washed and dried the dishes, Andrea put them away where Ian indicated. Intrigue aside, there was something warm and homey about being with these two. She had missed too much of that with her own parents.

"You must show Andrea your studio," Carla said when they had finished in the kitchen. "She would like to do a profile of you for *Kaleidoscope,* but didn't want to take advantage of asking since she is your guest. She thinks you may feel imposed on because so much already has been written about you."

"There's no such thing as too much publicity, as long as it isn't derogatory," Ian said. "Come. I'll show you the rest of the house and then we'll go up to the studio."

The other rooms of the house were also Spartan in their furnishings. "I have to keep it simple," Ian explained, "because of the proximity to the ocean. I can't afford to keep many things of value here that can't be quickly removed when the hurricanes sweep through."

"Is there a lot of damage here in hurricane season?"

"Not too much in the sheltered parts. Most of the houses aren't in the same danger as mine. Here on this jutting stretch of beach, a bad storm can take it all away. Usually, there's enough advance warning before a hurricane hits, but once," he said, wincing, "I had to rebuild the entire house."

"You should move farther inland," Carla suggested.

"If the sea weren't both my fascination and my means of earning a living, I suppose I would have long ago." He shrugged. "As it is, I make my uneasy peace with the sea. There are some mornings at high tide when I awaken to hear the ocean tapping at my door."

The studio, as Andrea had suspected,

was on the top floor, with the big glass wall overlooking the Atlantic. The stairs went directly up into the room without a preliminary landing or hall, like stairs to an attic. She was struck again by the neatness and order. There was no clutter, either of paint or canvas, and the huge windows, shining clean, admitted the light. An easel with a partially finished painting was positioned to catch the light. Brushes were cleaned and paints laid out in an orderly manner on a work-table. Wooden frames held stacks of completed canvases. Andrea needed no invitation to look through them.

"Ghosts," she said, looking intently at one painting. "These not-quite-seen images in the fog, are they intentional, or is it that I think I see them, the way one sees shapes in clouds?"

Ian came to stand over her, looking down at the painting. "No, what you see in this particular one is intentional. They represent the victims of land pirates who operated along the Jersey Shore."

"Land pirates? What are they?"

"Were. In the early history of the shore, it was not uncommon for the less humane of the settlers to prey upon ships. A group of these pirates would band together when a ship was expected, especially on stormy nights, and set out lanterns to simulate lighthouses. When the ship had been lured to a sandbar and beached, this band of murderers would board it, steal the cargo, and kill the crew and passengers."

Andrea shuddered. "Fact or legend?"

"Fact, sadly. Our ancestors weren't always wonderful people, as history would have us believe. . . . Here, you go ahead and look through these. I hear the telephone downstairs."

"It's for you, Carla," he called up seconds later. "Lydia Markum. She wants to know if you will be needing her tonight."

Andrea, left alone when Carla went to take the telephone call, continued to look through the paintings. She gasped in astonishment, her hands trembling, when she held up the last in the stack. It was of a woman, posed against the sea. A storm tossed the waves behind her, the wind blew tendrils of red-gold hair around her face. Even through the characteristic mist, Andrea could see herself in the painting. Was this the murdered girl Ian had said he would have liked to have known better? If Cheryl had posed for this painting, it was small wonder people had reacted to Andrea as they had yesterday. Then, in the lower right corner, she saw the date. It had been painted twenty-six years ago.

Thoroughly perplexed, she returned the painting to the stack. Then she heard Ian's returning steps on the stairs.

"Some of my very early work, pictures that have never been shown, are back there behind the chest if you'd like to see them," he told her.

Andrea moved over to look at these, and began flipping through the stack. One jumped out at her, and as she held it up to the light, she realized she was holding a painting of the house in her nightmare. It was all there, exactly as she had dreamed it—the rotting widow's walk falling away, the broken door standing open. Undulating, evil shapes moved through the mists that surrounded it. The only difference was that in this painting there was no Jersey Devil riding the moon.

Chapter Four

"I don't know. It's certainly a strange coincidence, isn't it?" Byron Standish, seated across from Andrea, was observing her with some skepticism.

This dinner date had not gotten off to quite the start she had hoped for. But the story she had told him would have made anybody skeptical. She wished she had kept quiet about what she had seen in Ian's studio, a painting of the house in her dream, a painting done years before the dream had occurred. She hadn't even told Carla or Ian. Why had she confided in this man whom she'd only just met?

A waiter came to the table and she was grateful for the diversion. She watched Byron as he ordered. In the muted light of the restaurant, he was even more handsome than last night in Carla's house. His eyebrows had a way of lifting expressively, bringing two distinct horizontal lines across his forehead. His dark hair was neatly clipped, and he wore his clothes with elegance. She could well imagine his impact in a courtroom.

What a dumb thing to do! she berated herself. She'd been an idiot to tell Byron about her dream and to connect it with a painting. She must have seemed as superstitious as those advocates of the Jersey Devil. She wondered if he might not be regretting having asked her out. Up to this point, he had seemed unsympathetic and more inclined to discount rather than credit the relationship of the vivid vision that marched through her sleeping mind and an old, unexhibited painting. But then his profession was one that was based on fact.

The waiter left, and she searched her mind for some topic that would change the subject away from her dream. Byron came to her rescue. "I did pull the file on that Kendexter case," he said. "People were right—there was very little investigation, as far as I could determine."

"Byron! Did you? What did you discover?" she asked, pulse quickening.

"To start with, her name wasn't Kendexter."

"She was using an alias?"

"No, not really. In fact, Cheryl herself may have believed Kendexter to be her name. From what sketchy details I did find, it appears she was born out near Leeds Point to a young woman named Lora Forge. Forge disappeared mysteriously and has never been heard from again." He took out a folded sheet of paper and glanced at it. "I made some notes. The Kendexter family took care of the child during the day while the mother worked as a dancer in Atlantic City. Lora disappeared after she left work one night, and since the child was still with her baby-sitters—the Kendexters—they kept her and raised her as their own."

"What were the Kendexters like? Would they have had anything to do with the mother's disappearance?"

"Hard to say. Probably not. They were friends of Lora's."

"It seems a little strange—the mother disappears and the girl is murdered. . . ."

"Not so much so when you consider the kind of people you're talking about. Forge and the Kendexters were on the shady side of the law, you might say."

"How so?"

"Both families were ne'er-do-wells, capable of petty thievery. Kendexter did two stretches in jail for stealing. And his wife was caught dealing drugs in a small-time way."

"But how would people like that have gotten custody of a child?"

"Nobody said they had official custody. The Child Welfare Department doesn't have a record of every child born. Some of them just fall through the system. In this case, Cheryl was left with the Kendexters by her natural mother. They moved away shortly after her disappearance to live in the community where you're staying. Chances are, they never mentioned this child to the authorities. Her natural background never came up until the murder investigation—what little there was."

"What was Cheryl like?"

He glanced again at his notes. "There's an old saying back where I come from that the apple doesn't fall far from the tree. With a background like hers, you wouldn't expect much."

"Was there any record of her being in trouble with the law?"

"She was a suspect several times, but she was never convicted of anything."

"Were there . . . photographs?"

He glanced up at her. "Yes. She was very beautiful, but we've established that since we know she looked like you." He said it lightly, looking straight into her eyes, but there was admiration too. She felt her earlier irritation at his lack of empathy vanish, and she looked down quickly at the table, a blush creeping up her cheeks.

"But she lacked your advantages, obviously." Glancing at his notes, he continued. "She dropped out of school after eighth grade, and, like her mother, went to work in an Atlantic City nightclub as a dancer. She was suspected of pushing drugs, but wasn't arrested. Suspected in a robbery once, but again, no arrest. She lived pretty much the way she was raised, I guess."

Jade. Tony. Her mind made the connection to the overdressed pair at Carla's party. Jade was a dancer. And hadn't Byron said something about there being criminals at the party? "Was anybody ever brought in as a serious suspect?" she asked.

"A few were questioned, but nothing came of it."

Andrea shook her head as if to clear away cobwebs. Given this girl's background, why would Ian have known her? And why would he have wished to know her better? His professional reputation made such a desired association seem unreal. There was a story there somewhere. She intended to pursue it.

"It's bothering you, isn't it?" Byron was observing her keenly.

"Yes," she admitted after a long pause. "It is. It's disconcerting to come to a new place, to be mistaken for someone who is dead, to. . . ." She stopped. She didn't want to mention Ian or his painting again.

"Small wonder it gave you bad dreams. That, and all the talk of the Jersey Devil."

"Don't equate my dream with superstition," she said, her irritation at his lack of understanding rising. "It was too real, and the painting depicted exactly the same house I had dreamed being inside."

He put his elbows on the table and looked at her. "Maybe it happened this way: You had a bad dream, and when you saw Gershner's painting, it reminded you in some way of the dream, and you just made the connection. The house and the dream became one."

"I know what I dreamed!" Andrea exclaimed. "It was all too vivid. And I know what I saw in the painting." Why was she so desperate to make him understand and sympathize with her?

He shrugged. "I won't pretend to understand. But here comes our dinner. Let's enjoy it—and deal with mysteries later." He smiled and reached across the table to touch her hand. At his touch, her irritation disappeared, replaced by warmth. "So tell me about your work," he continued. "You already have your own column in a magazine. Not bad."

"Well, a lot of it had to do with being in the right place at the right time." She told him about her work on a city daily, a job she'd gotten straight from college, and of going from there to *Kaleidoscope.* As they talked, she sensed there was a kindness and an honesty about him, although his work, out of necessity, must bring on a great deal of disillusionment about the goodness of human nature.

"And what about you?" Andrea asked finally. "You told me you came here only recently. Where were you before?"

"Philadelphia, by way of West Virginia. I grew up on a farm on the Kanawha River."

She stared across at this impeccably groomed man, trying to see him as a farm boy, and failed. "You don't have a trace of—"

"A mountaineer's accent?" He grinned. "Law school was pretty thorough. I had a professor who was a bear about speech and diction. 'You'll never be any better than the way you present yourself,' he said to me more than once." His eyes were distant with remembering. "I owe a lot to that man."

"So where does Philadelphia enter in?"

"I was in the D.A.'s office there briefly," he said, laughing. "When I was a kid growing up, if an old-timer wanted to pay a man a compliment, he'd say, 'He sounded like a Philadelphia lawyer,' or 'He looked like a Philadelphia lawyer.' I grew up with the idea that to be one was the epitome of everything. I guess a Philadelphia lawyer was the thing I wanted to be from the time I first heard the expression. Strange the things that influence a kid."

"But you changed your mind?"

"I changed my mind. The courts there are crowded beyond belief. All you're doing, or hope to be doing, is processing statistics. I got an offer to come out here and jumped at it."

As they continued to talk, the tension between them vanished, replaced by an easy camaraderie. She could visualize the child he had been, a boy growing up in a rustic area with his vision already firmly fixed on the world beyond. A world he hoped to better as he bettered himself. *I like you, Byron Standish,* she thought. *I like you a lot.*

When they were having coffee, Byron, glancing at another table across the room, half rose, then looked at her apologetically. Following his glance, she saw that Jade Stone and Tony Bandelli were seated there. Tony was beckoning to Byron.

"Do you mind? I'll just be a minute."

"Not at all. Go ahead."

He excused himself, and she watched him hurry across the room and seat himself beside them. He leaned forward and soon the trio was in intense conversation.

What business can he possibly have with that flashy pair? Andrea wondered. She recalled what Jade had said to her, "You're not interested in writing a series about the Jersey Shore. You came to stir up that old murder." Why would Jade care? Why the secrecy? If they had wanted to speak to Byron, why didn't they just come over to his table? There were only questions. No answers.

He was apologetic when he returned, but he made no attempt to explain. When they were on their way out, they passed a secluded booth. Feeling someone's eyes on her, Andrea glanced back to be confronted by the sight of Antonia and Frank. Both were watching her intently: Frank insolently, and Antonia with an expression that bordered on hate.

Chapter Five

"So, would you like to share my fire, sit in the studio, or go for a walk on the beach?"

Andrea hesitated, standing in Ian's doorway. Carla had set up this appointment for her, but she had not been able to come with her. Andrea felt a little guilty. Carla, and Ian as well, had thought this interview was to be slanted toward an article she would write on the painter's work. It wasn't.

Something bothered her, and she wanted to find out what it was. Something at an elemental level insisted that there was a correlation here—there were too many coincidences, too much mystery.

"A walk on the beach would be nice. I've seen very little of the seashore."

"I'll get my jacket. I see you're already dressed for outdoors." He glanced at her cape. "It's a nice day, but here by the water, there's an undercurrent of cold, even in the sun."

He returned quickly, an old Navy jacket over his sweater, smiling as he took her elbow. "This way. If we start off to the right, I can show you one of the wilder stretches of beach on this island."

The sand underfoot made walking difficult. After her first awkward steps, he looked down at her feet. She had worn low heeled pumps. "You didn't come shod for the sand, even if you are insulated against the cold. The sand will skin those shoes badly. You can still opt for the fire."

"Maybe later. I'm willing to give up these old shoes for a walk along the ocean. It's so very beautiful out here."

As they walked away from the house, down a stretch where tall grass and scrub pines grew, the sense of isolation was overwhelming. It was as if they had come to the end of the world, and there was no other. Yet she knew that only a block or so behind them, beyond the dunes and twisted pines, lay the long, close cluster of houses, the streets and avenues that made up Ocean City.

They came out of the scrubby growth to a stretch of deserted beach. "The summer people have gone home," he told her. "We'll have this all to ourselves—and the sea gulls too." In the sunshine, the white sand dazzled Andrea, and the water stretched beyond, blue into infinity. It was a world strange to her, yet she felt its elemental magnetism.

"It gets to you, doesn't it?" Ian asked, watching her. "There's some spirit of the sea that's like nothing else in the world, and once experienced, it won't let you go."

"Have you always lived by the sea, Ian?"

"Always. Beside it, or on it."

She turned toward him with an inquisitive look.

"I was in the Navy for a while," he explained. "Joined up while I was a kid."

"And before that, you lived here?"

"Not here in Ocean City, but near." A closed, private expression crossed his face and he turned away, walking off in front of her, striding along the beach.

"Wait for me," Andrea called, deliberately making her voice light. "I can't keep up in this sand." She knew that in asking about his early life, she had trespassed on some private space. But if she were to find answers, she must persist without seeming to probe.

"Sorry." Ian turned to wait, gallantly holding out his hand. "What a sight we must make," he said. "An old sailor and you, an autumn child in your long cloak, walking hand in hand on this windy beach."

"Why do you call me an autumn child?"

He looked at her thoughtfully. "I don't know. I suppose it's because you remind me of an autumn child I once knew."

"Was she important to you?"

"Once was. Yes, very."

"Cheryl Kendexter?"

"No. I barely knew Cheryl."

"Were you married once, Ian?"

He released her hand. "Is this an interview about my professional work, or an attempt to invade my privacy?"

"I'm sorry," Andrea said instantly.

"It's all right." He stooped to pick up a shell from the sand. "I've always been too touchy with journalists who are bent on invading private places."

"Places you won't let anyone in?"

"They have nothing to do with my art."

"Everything we do, everything we are, influences our art, whatever its medium."

"Profound statement from one so young."

"I'm right, though—aren't I?"

He held up the shell, examining it minutely before dropping it into his pocket. "I suppose you are, but I insist upon being judged only for the end results, not the way I got there."

Andrea, with a reporter's instinct of knowing when to back off and when to move in, changed the subject. "The sea is so calm and beautiful today. It's hard to imagine it wild and raging the way you sometimes paint it."

"It has many moods. Just when you think it's your friend, it can turn on you with devastating abruptness, taking away from you all you value. Come on. Let's sit on this hump of dune grass and share a bit of solitude—while the sea is our friend."

She watched him covertly. Mid-forties, she would guess. Younger than

Carla, but not by much. She wondered what bond they shared. Carla was open, but with an air of lazy elegance, and Ian was secretive one minute, genial and outgoing the next. She sensed unprobed depths in him, and possibly a capability for strength as violent as the storms of his seascapes. What was the secret that he held so close and refused to confide?

"You don't have a notebook," he observed in an almost accusatory tone.

"Notebook? No, I don't."

"But you came to interview me, or so I thought."

"I suppose I left it in the car."

"Or is it that you didn't come to interview me? Only to pry?" But a moment later he reached over and squeezed her hand apologetically. "I shouldn't have said that. Don't look so stricken. Reporters sometimes make me paranoid."

"You don't have your sketchbook, either. Why don't we walk back and get them both, and I can watch you work?" Andrea suggested.

"Fair enough. I had meant to capture something of this day, anyway."

Minutes later, with the tools of their trades in hand, they returned to the tufted dune and sat again. Ian sketched the beach, where a sandpiper foraged among the shells and a pair of boats glided across the glossy surface of the sea far off in the distance.

Andrea glanced at his work from time to time. He worked quickly, expertly, doing numerous versions in the sketchbook, tearing them off and laying them on the sand, weighted against the wind with a small smooth stone. He appeared unaware of her existence.

She worked also, jotting down observations to use when writing the next article in her series. Her mind was far removed from that present project, however. She thought instead of the portrait of the girl in the mist, a picture that might have been painted of herself, and of an old house empty of people whom she didn't know. How could she get this enigmatic man to open up and talk to her?

So quickly that she had not seen the change coming on, clouds built up, throwing shadows that ran along the beach. The sky turned gray and the ocean assumed a leaden look.

"What did I tell you about the sea and

its changing moods?" Ian asked. "Look how quickly the sun is obscured and the storm clouds pile up."

Andrea stood up, closing the notebook and drawing her cape close against the cold that had come on. Ian, still seated, looked up at her, his eyes fixed in an intent stare.

"Why are you looking at me like that?" she asked.

"I was wondering if you would pose for me. Would you?"

She nodded. "Of course. I'd be flattered."

"Walk down that way toward the water, turn toward me, and let your cape go in the wind." He was already preparing a new page.

She walked to the edge of the water, posing as he had asked, letting the wind billow the folds of her cape and whip her hair across her face. She wondered if he had made any connection between her and the girl he had painted so long ago. For Andrea, too, might have been the model for that other portrait in the mist.

Behind her the waves lapped at the shore, the sea gulls screamed and dipped overhead, and there seemed nothing visible on the horizon other than the beach and twisted pine trees. She felt a chill of apprehension. A girl who had looked like her had died three years ago in a place as deserted as this. And nobody had cared enough about her, according to Byron, to follow through with any real investigation. Byron. The thought of him erased the faint sense of doom. Last night, at Carla's door, when he had brought her home, he had reached out, holding her by both shoulders. "Take care," he had said softly. "Don't let any of this upset you. It's all a coincidence." And then he had leaned forward and kissed her gently on the lips. As she looked deep in his eyes, Andrea had been sure she saw more than just friendly intent.

As he drove away, she had stood at the door, unwilling to move while she still felt the lingering sensation of the kiss, the scent of his skin. She realized how attracted she was to Byron, despite his seeming penchant for secrecy. He had been politely evasive when she had attempted to ask about his connection with Jade and Tony. He hadn't seen Frank and Antonia, but when she mentioned them, Byron said only that he knew Frank from some work he had done with his father's and his assistance. Frank's father was a town policeman. *Too close to the law for the law to investigate*—hadn't Lydia said something like that?

"I said you can come back now!" Ian's shouted invitation brought Andrea back to the present. "You were off in another world," he said when she walked up to where he was seated. "That's the third time I called you. Well, what do you think?" He held out the sketch he had made of her.

She took the picture from him and looked at it a long time. He had pictured her as a sort of goddess of the sea. Her cape swirled about her, part reality, part mist, part water. "It's lovely," she said at last. "But I don't think it's a sketch of me. I think you painted this once before, a long time ago. Is that offer to share your fire still valid? I'm freezing."

Inside, seated on the sofa, she watched Ian draw back the fire screen, pile on more logs, and stir them to blazing warmth. "I can offer you tea, coffee, or hot chocolate. Which will it be?" he asked.

"Hot chocolate would be nice."

"Hot chocolate it is." He left to go to the kitchen, and she stared into the leaping flames, thinking her day had been nice—but wasted. She had no more answers than before she came, only more questions.

He returned shortly with two of the big yellow mugs he had used to serve their tea in yesterday. "Here—rich, hot, and sweet. And lots of whipped cream. Skoal!"

She drank the chocolate, grateful for the warmth, and looked again at the sketch. "Ian, who were you thinking of when you did this? It's me, and yet it isn't. You were trying to capture the essence of someone else, weren't you?"

"Yes, I suppose I was." He took the sketch from her and looked at it as if it had been done by somebody else, and he had never seen it before.

"Who?"

"My daughter. If she were alive. If things had been . . . different."

Chapter Six

Andrea arrived at Carla's house to find another car parked in the driveway. Randolph's red Buick! She hurried into the house to find Randolph, his wife, Jeannie, and Carla waiting for her.

"Well!" Randolph said, after their initial greetings. "I read the fax copy of your article this morning. What's this about your coming upon a murder mystery?"

Andrea laughed. "I thought that might bring out the investigative reporter in you—and bring you both here!"

"And you were right. I think it's worth looking into."

"But hardly a story for *Kaleidoscope?*"

"*Anything's* a story for *Kaleidoscope.* And imagine what it would do for us if we solved the crime!" Randolph said excitedly.

"And it would be a public service

too," Jeannie said. "An unsolved murder means a murderer is on the loose."

"That too. Tell me all you know about it," Randolph commanded.

"That the victim looked like me, that people around here believe in the devil. Some of them think I'm here to investigate the crime, and some of them apparently think *I* am the dead girl."

Jeannie and Randolph looked at her in amazement.

"It's true." She told them the details—what few details she knew—plus the information that an assistant district attorney was to stop by later with a photograph of Cheryl.

"That nice young Byron Standish?" Carla asked. "Invite him to stay for dinner. We'll make a party of it."

"Where did you meet Byron?" Andrea asked, remembering that he was not from this area.

"When I first met him, he was a young lawyer in the office of our attorney in Philadelphia. Benton recommended him to one of his friends at the courthouse here. Come to think of it, why don't I call Ian and invite him too? How did your interview with him go, by the way?"

Andrea shrugged. "Interesting. I like him a lot, but he's so secretive that it would be impossible to get any new information about him." She wanted to ask Carla if she knew anything about Ian's daughter, but decided this was not the time.

"I'd like to see where this crime took place," Randolph said. "Is it near here?"

"It's a so-called gravel pit, out on Point Road," Carla answered.

"Do you know how to find it?"

"I know where it is," Carla told him. "It's just an overgrown area along the roadside."

"Let's go."

"Let's wait for Byron," Andrea suggested. "He was to bring the photo first thing after work, and it's after five now."

Carla, who had been seated on the sofa, legs tucked under, stood up. "Too late to ask Lydia now. I guess you people will have to make do with my cooking."

"But you hate to cook," Andrea protested, feeling contrite.

"Not half as much as I hate eating alone," Carla told her with a humorous twinkle in her eyes. "It may not be edible, but I'm willing to make it just to keep you young people here. And as for you, young man," she said, turning to Randolph, "you two aren't going to drive back home tonight. I have plenty of room in this house and you and Jeannie haven't been to visit since I moved here."

Randolph smiled at her affectionately. He was a tall, thin, blond man with an intensity of purpose about him, and Andrea was surprised to see him reach out and envelop Carla in a firm hug. He had seldom displayed any emotion in the years she had known him, beginning when he had begun dating her Bryn Mawr roommate.

But Carla had that effect on people—there was something so sweet and unassuming about her. Andrea hoped again that something was developing between Carla and Ian. She liked them both, even given Ian's fierce protection of his privacy. He had no sooner mentioned a daughter earlier today than he had refused to discuss her any further.

"Carla, why don't I start dinner while you phone the friend you were going to invite?" Jeannie asked. "I *love* to cook, and I'm sure I can find things in your kitchen."

"You're an angel, Jeannie. Andrea, I think you know your way around the kitchen well enough to show her, don't you?"

Andrea was glad to have some time alone with Jeannie. They hurried off to the kitchen. Following her friend's plump, bouncy figure, Andrea decided Jeannie hadn't changed in any way at all since college. She and Randolph were proof that opposites can attract successfully. Jeannie, with her short dark curls, impulsive chatter, and open friendliness, was such a contrast to Randolph that Andrea laughed aloud.

"What's so funny?" Jeannie turned her head and grinned over her shoulder.

"I was thinking of the first time Randolph came to the dorm to take you out. I thought, 'Oh, brother! They're so different, they'll be at each other's throats before the date ends.' But look what happened!"

"Yes, look at us now. So, who is this lawyer who's stopping by? Is it social or business?"

Andrea felt herself blush. Jeannie, for all her surface frivolity, had a way of bringing the emotions of others into sharp focus. "A little of both, I hope," she admitted.

Jeannie observed her a minute longer, her bright eyes questioning, anticipating confidence.

"I don't know him well enough to say—yet. But I'm very attracted to him, yes."

"Well, we'll just have to wait and see, then." Jeannie knew to change the subject. "What shall we make a meal of? Carla's a vegetarian, you know, like you."

"Oh, is she? I didn't know that!" Andrea realized for the first time that no meat had been served at any meal, either here or at Ian's. She was glad to find another common link with her hostess. "In that case, I'll be in my element. I can make a great deep-dish casserole with peppers, mushrooms, onions, cheese, and tomato sauce."

"Sounds like pizza."

"Well, the topping side of one, anyway."

"Okay, that'll be the main dish. I'll use

these potatoes to make a cream soup." Jeannie opened the refrigerator. "We need a yellow vegetable."

"How about this squash?" Andrea asked, retrieving a large butternut from the bin under the counter.

"Perfect—my soup, your casserole, the squash cubed and baked with lots of butter, cinnamon, and some honey, and I'll use these strawberries to make a mousse for dessert."

"I may never let you girls go home," Carla said, coming into the kitchen in time to hear Jeannie's authoritative dictation of the dinner menu. "What may I do?"

"Go sit," Andrea said. "Is Ian coming?"

"Yes. Said he'd be delighted. So there'll be six of us, counting your young man."

Jeannie cast a swift glance at Andrea. "Are you holding something out on me? *Your young man?*"

"Wishful thinking on Carla's part. Maybe mine too," she admitted, thinking of last night's kiss.

Ian arrived shortly, filling the house with his big, cheerful presence. He was avidly interested in all phases of Randolph's new publication, and the two men, along with Carla, retreated to the living room.

Andrea, working in the kitchen with Jeannie, realized how keenly she missed having a family. An empty apartment was not all that wonderful to go home to when the workday was over. Had she simply been postponing living, or had she been too busy to do anything about it?

Byron arrived at the kitchen door at that moment, interrupting her bemused self-analysis. Once again Andrea was stirred by his handsome good looks. *Wishful thinking indeed!* she thought as she greeted him and introduced Jeannie.

Byron shook Jeannie's hand and gave Andrea a folder. "I warn you, it may be a shock," he said.

It was. The photograph was a head shot, almost life-size, taken close-up, and in color. There was too much of herself in the photograph. It wasn't logical. It simply wasn't sane that nature could have created two unrelated people and made them look so identical.

Wordlessly, she handed the photograph to Jeannie. "But, Andrea, there must be some mistake. This is a photograph of you," Jeannie exclaimed.

Carla, Ian, and Randolph walked in and gathered around the picture. "That's Cheryl, not Andrea," Ian said quietly but firmly.

"If we're going to view the site," Byron said in response to Randolph's suggestion, "we'd better go right away. It'll soon be too dark to see anything—not that there's going to be anything to see years later. Coming with us, Andrea?"

She hesitated. The idea of viewing the scene of the crime gave her an eerie feeling. She picked up the photo again. This was not a picture of her. The light brown eyes that stared from the print were not her own. This was someone named Cheryl Kendexter and she was dead. *Doppelgänger.* She had heard Lydia mutter that word the night she had first come face-to-face with Andrea. She shook her head. All this talk of spirits and the devil—she couldn't let it influence her. To do so would be to give in to superstition. "Yes, I'll come," she answered.

It was decided that the young people

would all go while Ian and Carla watched the dinner to make sure it didn't overcook. "We'll take my car," Byron offered. "I can find the site easily. I took a run out there yesterday after I looked at the file. The place is a kind of lovers' lane. Couples park there at night."

"Was it ever considered that the crime might have been the result of a lovers' quarrel, then? A boyfriend who might have killed her?" Randolph asked.

"A couple of guys were brought in for questioning, but both had airtight alibis. She had a reputation for playing the field."

Andrea could see why it was called the gravel pit. A scarred area of gouged-out earth, there was about an acre or two of land where gravel had been taken, leaving depressions in places, mounds in others. Over the years, scrub pines and brush had grown up, covering the mounds. Where gravel still lay, there were intricate trails moving in and out around the pit.

"Ideal parking spot for couples," Randolph remarked. "A dozen cars could come in here and still have privacy from the others."

"Ideal place to become a victim of crime too," Byron said. "The place is like a jungle with all that growth of pines. According to my notes, over here is where the body was found."

They followed him as he climbed up a steep mound of earth and down the other side. The loose, sandy soil was banked high on one side of a pit that was littered with the debris of recent dumping.

Jeannie moved over close to Andrea, taking her arm, as if to comfort her for some unexplainable loss. Andrea stared at the spot, feeling the cold prickle of a chill move up and down her back. She could imagine too keenly the horror of dying there alone in the garbage-littered darkness. She could almost feel herself gasping for one more last breath.

"Certainly isolated out here." Randolph looked around. "No other houses. Well, there is a big one back there behind the trees. . . ." He pointed in the direction of a house that sat farther up the road, most of it concealed by shrubbery.

"That's the Bentleys' house," Andrea told him.

"Very upper crust," Byron added. "Old family, old money. Simon Bentley is involved in politics in this end of the state."

"Were they questioned? Did anyone ask them if they'd heard anything unusual?" Randolph asked.

"Briefly, from what I read in the report. The daughter was home alone. She stated that there are always night noises from down here—car radios and such. She said there was nothing out of the ordinary."

They took a last cursory tour of the place and returned to the car. Byron agreed to Randolph's request that he make available what details there were of the investigation. The blue curtain of dusk had fallen rapidly during the time they had been here, and by the time they emerged to the side of the road, the landscape was almost in total darkness.

"I can't believe it's night already," Randolph said.

"A few more days and it will be pitch-dark before now," Byron remarked. "The time changes this weekend."

"That always confuses me," Jeannie said. "I never know which time you set the clock ahead, and which back."

"That's easy," Byron told her. "Spring forward, fall back."

"I'll remember—" She froze, grabbing Andrea's arm. "Look! Somebody's at the car!"

A running shadow fled before their approach, and farther away a car started up and was gone into the darkness before they could reach their automobile. Two additional cars, driving slowly, went out in the same direction.

"Shouldn't we follow it?" Jeannie asked.

"We wouldn't know which car we're following—there are three of them. Probably it was just someone intending an illicit rendezvous," Byron said.

"But why get out and check your car?"

"They may have wanted to know who caught them—or almost did."

Plausible explanation aside, Andrea felt a sense of foreboding. Surely the incident wouldn't have had anything to do with a three-year-old murder. But it *felt* as if it did.

Once they had returned to the house, however, it was impossible not to be lighthearted in the company of the others. Carla and Ian had the table set, festive with candles and a bowl of bright chrysanthemums. Andrea and Jeannie served the dinner, and at Carla's suggestion, they put the mystery aside to talk about more pleasant things and enjoy one another's company.

After dinner they gathered around the library fireplace. There, apparently made mellow by the rapport, and taking an instinctive liking to Randolph, Ian began to open up about his past.

Andrea had triggered this by telling the others about the sketch he had done of her. "Ian . . ." she said hesitantly, "there's a painting in your studio, a picture *I* might have posed for, but it's dated twenty-six years ago. Who was she?" She watched the light and shadows from the fire flicker across his face. He stared at her thoughtfully, as if in looking at her, he was seeing this woman from the past again.

"Her name was Lora," he said. "When I painted the picture, her name was Lora Gershner."

Andrea gasped, remembering what Byron had said about a woman named Lora being Cheryl's natural mother. Byron, too, had stopped talking to Jeannie in midsentence and turned his attention to Ian.

Ian stroked his beard thoughtfully and seemed to look at them in almost mute appeal. Finally he spoke. "I know you're journalists, Andrea and Randolph, but what I'm about to say is not for print. It has nothing to do with my work. If it may help to solve this case, I'm willing to tell it, but I want you both to promise it's off the record. Agreed?"

Randolph and Andrea gave their word that nothing Ian said would be used in any story they wrote, without his consent.

"What you first have to understand is that I was born into poverty more abject than any of you can imagine. My mother and I lived out near Leeds Point. My dad had been a fisherman, but he was lost at sea when I was quite young. My mother did the best she could, I suppose, but she lacked education, initiative, and, I always thought, common sense. We lived in a hovel, and if there was a penny ahead from her odd jobs, it was owed before it came in.

"Understandably," he went on, "given that background, I was the playground outcast. I found early on that I had a natural ability to draw pictures of the sea, the boats, and the men who worked the shore. I also learned that when drawing, I was transported out of myself, my misery, and all the squalor. I could be anybody I wanted to be in my imagination. Art was an escape from my loneliness."

"And so your enormous talent was born of privation," Carla murmured.

"What talent I have was born of misery—yes. The only other people who were equally down and out were a family named Setter. An entire tribe of them—grandparents, sons, daughters, grandchildren, cousins, maybe four generations—lived in a big, old, ruined house, also near Leeds Point. Lora was my age, a granddaughter in the family. I can see now that our early friendship was based on nothing more than the truth of the old adage: 'misery loves company.' "

He paused, his gaze fixed on the fire. Andrea felt an overwhelming sympathy. Life had not been fair to this good man.

"Our alliance was an early one, and by our midteens, I was in love with Lora, or thought I was. We were subsequently married, and I, determined to pull us out of the rut we had grown up in, joined the Navy. I knew this was my only hope of getting an education. By that time, my mother had died, and I had only Lora.

"So I went to sea, and Lora remained behind. Had I loved her less, I might have noticed flaws in her character. I can look at it now, from the distance of years, and recall her selfishness and instability. Lora could never maintain a lasting interest in any one thing. Today's goal would be gone tomorrow. It may have been the environment she came from, or it may have been in her genes—I don't know. It's a strange thing about poverty: It can give some a drive to overcome, while it pulls others down to lower depths.

"The fact of the matter is, as time went on, her letters became infrequent and full of complaints. Before my enlistment term was completed, Lora had asked for and obtained a divorce to marry a man named Steven Forge."

Andrea reached out and grasped

Byron's arm. "Cheryl's mother!" Lora Setter Gershner Forge—she was the woman in the painting in Ian's studio, the mother of the murdered girl.

Ian glanced at her and nodded. "Yes. I came home, went to college, and my painting began to earn my living. I had lost touch with Lora. It wasn't until reading about Cheryl's death that I made the connection and realized the young woman was most surely my daughter."

A gasp of astonishment came from the group around the fire.

"You see, I'd met Cheryl briefly. She had responded to an ad I placed for an artist's model, but given that name, I never made the connection. Because there was something about her that reminded me of my former wife, I used her to pose on occasion. But—and I say this sadly—there was something hard and unsettling about the girl. She never seemed a person you could wholly trust. . . ."

"According to the police report," Byron said, "Cheryl was the daughter of Steven Forge. Why don't you think she was born of that marriage?"

"From the age she gave me. From the

age published in the newspapers too. She would have been born while I was at sea, but still married to Lora."

Carla, seated near Ian, reached over and took his hand wordlessly. The group was still seated mute and pensive when the phone rang, the jangle loud in the silence.

"It's for you, Andrea," Carla said seconds later.

Andrea stepped out to the hall and picked up the receiver. "Hello?"

For an instant there was only silence at the other end, and then it came: a high, thin, eerie shriek. No words. Just a voice that could not be of this world, screaming and screaming.

Chapter Seven

Andrea fingered the keyboard of her word processor. The story eluded her. Mainly, she told herself, it was because she wasn't sure of what she wanted to write about. A follow-up on Cheryl's murder? That was what Randolph really wanted—to reactivate interest in the crime. But she didn't know anything more about that mystery now than she had in the beginning, except that Cheryl had been Ian's daughter.

But that was Ian's secret, and it could not be told without his permission. Still, she continued to imagine the headline: BODY FOUND IN GRAVEL PIT WAS DAUGHTER OF FAMOUS ARTIST. She was willing to bet more effort would have gone into solving the crime if Cheryl's true identity had been known.

How sad to have lived on the outer fringe of society and never to have had the advantages Ian could have given her.

No doubt, had her identity been known, she would also still be alive. Hers had been a style of living that was not conducive to longevity. People who were of criminal intent were likely to step on the toes of someone else of criminal intent—often with lethal results.

Surely it was sad for Ian too. What must it be like to realize one had a daughter all these years, but not to know of it until she was dead? Andrea could understand all the reasons Ian would want it kept quiet now. And they had met casually, and neither had known. It seemed very strange.

Strange was also the word for the phone call she had received last night. Andrea was still not persuaded, as were the others, that it was merely some Halloween prankster. Why had the caller asked for her by name? And how many people here knew her name, anyway? Most of those she had met had been disturbed by her marked resemblance to Cheryl. *That's it!* she thought with sudden insight. It was Cheryl's killer, determined to drive her away. It had been someone who was superstitious enough to believe in the occult and to view her as some threatening spirit of revenge.

Andrea got up and paced around the room. This reasoning made her realize that she could also be in danger. She went to the kitchen, made a cup of tea, and tried again to write. Still no story line. Randolph and Jeannie had gone back to Philadelphia, but with a promise to return tomorrow. Carla had gone shopping. There was something disquieting about being left alone here, but she really didn't want to venture into town, either, considering the kind of attention she had gotten the first day.

She took out her map of the area and unfolded it. Of course there were other places she could go to gather material on the Jersey Shore, such as Leeds Point. The name shimmered on the map and intrigued her—Leeds Point. Home of the Jersey Devil, a creature born of human fear, guilt, and ignorance. Leeds Point, home of the "Setter tribe," as Ian had characterized them. And home of Ian Gershner, poverty's child, now a famous artist. Leeds Point. The more she thought about it, the more she was compelled to go and see it for herself.

Less than an hour later, she pulled off the road and parked opposite an old school in a village called Oceanville. She had not come this route before, and she checked her map again to make sure she was headed in the right direction. "Right," she said aloud, tracing her position. She had already come through Pleasantville, Absecon, Absecon Heights, and now was in Oceanville. She saw from the map that Leeds Point lay only a short distance beyond.

Andrea returned the map to the glove compartment and sat for a minute longer, looking around her. It had rained the night before, and the last of the leaves were rapidly falling, leaving bare trees to lift dark branches to the sky. Only the pines still whispered of summer.

She glanced in the rearview mirror preparatory to getting back on the highway. No traffic was coming in either direction. Only one other car was in sight, pulled off the road far back. She continued on her way for a short distance before she realized she was bearing left, away from the sea. It didn't make sense. Ian had certainly grown up near the water, and the Setters as well. And that old ruined house—if there was such a place in reality—overlooked the ocean.

When she had traveled for some time, taking roads and trails leading right, she realized she was lost. The Atlantic, as designated on the map, pushed in between the islands to become Great Bay just to the right of Leeds Point. Lost or not, if she just continued. . . .

Rounding a bend where pines obscured the landscape, she came upon the house so suddenly that it took her a minute to focus on the ruin. And when she knew what it was, it was as if her mind refused to register, and her heart stopped.

The windows were boarded up as if in a futile effort to salvage the wreckage of what surely once had been a grand, proud house. There was not even a shadow of doubt that this was the house in Ian's painting, and it was the same house she had wandered through in her nightmare.

It sat alone in a weed- and brush-grown lot. Out beyond, the scrub pines marched in low, twisted growth. Toward the front, a ravaged stretch of beach separated it from the bay. She parked the car on the weed-choked trail between the house and the water and sat, looking up at it.

Unpainted for years, the boards had darkened to a near-black patina. Beyond the sagging veranda a door lay open, inviting the elements, wild things, and trespassers. The widow's walk, drooping precariously, seemed fixed to the building by nothing more substantial than a gossamer thread.

Some urge impelled her forward. She got out of the car, closing the door quietly, as if expecting any sound to bring hordes swooping down upon her. Pine branches reached out and needled her face as she entered the walkway to the porch. Should she risk going inside? Would anyone care?

She wondered suddenly if Ian ever came back to this place, to the site of his lonely beginning and defeats, where his considerable talent had been born. Why had he painted a picture of this house and put it away, never to be exhibited? Child of poverty who had moved away, what secrets did he have that held him here?

Andrea stepped tentatively up on the

porch. Inside, the rooms, with their boarded-up windows, were dark. A drift of brown pine needles lay beyond the door. What else might be lurking there? Fear made her hesitate, but a desire to go inside overcame timidity.

In the dark interior an acrid odor assailed her. Years of disuse, mold, and decay had seeped into the timbers. She tested the floor gingerly. It seemed solid enough, yet instinct told her this was not the place to be all alone, when no one knew where she was. She should have left a note for Carla. Suppose she had an accident, or suppose something fell. . . .

The urge to flee this place was suddenly as compelling as the one to enter had been. *Just a little farther and I'll leave,* she thought. There was a room back there—she *knew* there was. She advanced slowly, giving her eyes a chance to grow accustomed to the darkness.

Doors creaked on rusted hinges and opened into empty rooms. Strips of wallpaper hung loose. Something scurried off, startling her, until reason assured her it was only some small creature running away on timorous feet, claws clicking against the bare boards of the floor.

Light from the front door did not reach the corridors in the back. Almost in total darkness, she felt her way, searching, determined to discover whether reality and her dream were the same. She stopped once, thinking, or feeling, rather, that something had come up behind her on silent feet. Something stealthy, like a breath caught and held. . . .

She stopped, listening. There was no sound, just a kind of pulse beat in the darkness, a vibration that disturbed the air. *There's a stairway back here somewhere,* she thought. She started walking again, inching forward, feeling the wall as she went. But the other presence moved with her. She could feel the disturbance of space, the clandestine movement.

She started to turn toward this presence, preparatory to flight, but arms reached out, encircling her. A hand closed over her scream, just before a blackness, darker than anything she had ever imagined, descended. Then it came again: that high shriek that had reached her over the telephone last night, a sound that might have been made by the devil himself.

Chapter Eight

Headache and intense hunger were Andrea's first sensations when she awoke, prodding at her even before fear. In her groggy, drug-induced awareness, fear seemed secondary. She tried to recall what had happened to her, knowing it was important to remember. How long ago had it been?

She struggled to sit up. Strangely, she was no longer bound and gagged, as she remembered. There was only a blindfold, a kind of elastic bandage, covering her eyes. Tearing it off, she saw that she was lying in the corner of a very small room. This was not the big house of her nightmare. This was obviously a tiny place, a cabin. The windows were bare, letting the sunshine pour in.

She held her wrist to check the time, but her watch had been broken. The crystal was smashed, leaving only one jagged corner of glass, and the hands of the watch were bent. Convinced that her captors were still with her, she stood up unsteadily, clutching at a windowsill as she rose.

How had they come to this place? Outside, there was only sunshine and low scrub pine trees that shimmered like undulating waves and went on and on forever. Dizziness overwhelmed her, and she slid gratefully back to the floor. If only she could reconstruct the previous day. . . .

Or had it been only a day ago? How long had she been here, unconscious? If she could force her brain to function, things might begin to make sense. If only she had a glass of water, or even better, a cup of coffee.

She racked her brain. She had been in the rear of that Halloweenlike house, looking for the stairs, or, rather, *feeling* for the stairs in the darkness, and someone had come up behind her. Was that it? Andrea dropped her head into her hands, thinking, trying to concentrate through the fog.

More than one person had attacked her. Their voices had been muffled, as though coming through a mask. They had overpowered her, bound and gagged her, and then came the long, horrible interval while they had simply stayed in that old house, awaiting darkness.

"Can't risk carrying her out in daylight," one had told the other. "We'll just have to wait it out until it's night."

"Did you bring the pills?" the other had asked.

"Yes, I have them. Enough to ensure a long, deep sleep."

After the interminable wait, Andrea had felt herself lifted and carried outside where she had been thrown carelessly into the trunk of a car.

"Better give her the pills now," a muffled voice had directed. "It'll keep her quiet so she won't bang on the trunk door."

The gag was removed then. With a hand still clamped over her mouth, the pills were forced into one side. "Swallow them if you want to make it easy. They're gelatin capsules and will melt anyway. Either way, they'll knock you out."

At the first dire taste of the melting capsule, she had swallowed hard. It had been almost her last memory, except she knew that they drove a long way, or so it seemed.

Now she listened intently. There was no sound that indicated anyone else was in the house with her. Who had brought her here? With the passing of her initial grogginess, a fear as intense as any she had ever felt before thrust at her. She had narrowly escaped being murdered. She might have been as easily killed as kidnapped!

Who? Why? It came to her then that it had something to do with Cheryl. People had reacted strangely to her from the first, and it was all because in their own minds they associated her with the dead woman who had looked so much like her.

"An unsolved murder means there's still a murderer on the loose." Jeannie had said that, and it was true. Now Andrea might soon be a victim. Someone had watched her and had followed her to that old house, and one of them had been the person who had made the phone call to her. That same Valkyrie shriek had terrified her there in the dark. Somebody viewed her as a threat, and that same person might be here now, lurking in this house, waiting to kill her!

She stood up again, fear making her more steady on her feet. She made a quick search of the house. She had been right—it was a cabin. Three small rooms, all empty, it sat in the midst of a growth of pines and sandy soil. The trees were low, as if some blight had passed over, dwarfing them for all time.

Then she realized where she was—in the South Jersey pine barrens, a stretch of wilderness that grew nothing but stunted, little more than waist-high pines. She had heard it was possible to be lost in this low wilderness and never be found again.

Her previous newspaper had done a series some years back on the efforts being made by environmentalists to save the pine barrens from encroaching civilization. Developers had hoped to build there. As she recalled, it had been quite a controversy at the time.

This cabin must belong to some long-gone inhabitant of the region, for people did live in this wilderness. She recalled that one news story had called them "pineys," a term that was equivalent to "hillbilly" in the Appalachian Mountains.

It occurred to her that to be abandoned here might be almost as dangerous as being dropped off in the desert. Who would find her? Could she ever find her own way out before fatigue or, more important, dehydration, overcame her? Was there water in the kitchen even if the cabin was abandoned?

Going into the next room to investigate, she found her purse lying on the counter. When she picked it up, she saw that her car keys were underneath. She opened the purse to find that a message had been left inside. Written on ruled tablet paper with letters printed in black crayon, so large that they filled both sides of the folded sheet, the note said:

> *This was a warning. Next time you won't be so lucky. Get out of here. Go back to where you came from and forget Cheryl Kendexter. Your car is at the end of the lane pointed in the direction to follow. Get in it and go. Don't look back. Don't come back or you will die.*

The last word had been emphasized both by size and underlining.

It was all the motivation she needed to leave this place behind. Was the note on the level, and she was free to go, or was there someone out there, playing a cat-and-mouse game with her? The only way to find out was to leave.

She hurried outside. After a quick look around, she decided that "lane" referred to the narrow path in front of the cabin. She was soon on it, running, stumbling headlong down its sandy length. As promised, her car was parked where the path widened and became a kind of abandoned, yet still passable road.

Utterly relieved when she turned the key and the engine came to life, she would have liked to speed away, but the stones and sand made for slow driving. It seemed forever before she reached a highway.

Andrea hesitated at this intersection. There was a gas station on the corner. That would mean a telephone—she could call the police and report her ordeal. Yet something told her to wait. She would go to Carla's first. She did go inside and ask directions, hoping her shaking would not be noticed.

"Stay the way you're headed now," the attendant said, looking at her curiously. "Keep on that road; it'll take you to Pleasantville." She thanked him hastily, knowing she could find her own way from there.

She hadn't driven long before she began to recognize landmarks from the day before—if it indeed had been yesterday when she came this way. Here was where she had turned off the main road to go toward the sea, the road that had led her so surprisingly up to that old house. Someone in front of her, but headed toward her, had on a turn signal for that direction now. The traffic light turned red and she stopped, watching the car turn in front of her. She did a double take. They hadn't seen her. Byron was driving, and Ian was seated beside him!

Chapter Nine

Jeannie, Randolph, and Carla were sitting at the kitchen table when Andrea arrived. "Where in the world have you been?" Jeannie asked, rushing toward her when Andrea burst into the room. "We were so worried!"

"Andrea, what is it?" Carla cried, alarm registering on her face at the sight of Andrea's dishevelment and white-faced terror. "Come over here and sit down!" Carla and Jeannie took her arm, leading her to a chair. Carla placed a cup of coffee in front of her. "Tell us what happened to you."

Quickly she told them about her experience while they listened, horror and consternation appearing on their faces.

"I knew something had to be terribly wrong when you didn't come home and it was getting late," Carla said. "I called Randolph on the off chance that you might have gone to Philadelphia for something."

"And when it got toward morning, and there was still no sign of you, Randy and I drove out here," Jeannie added. "We've been up all night."

"I thought at first you might have had a date with Byron," Carla said, "until he called here asking for you. . . ."

"Byron called? When was that?"

"Around ten o'clock last night."

"Carla, I saw Byron and Ian going out in the direction of that old house this morning, and—"

Carla looked at her shrewdly. "Yes, they were. They left here not long ago to go there to look for you. I see what you're thinking, but Byron came as soon as he knew you were missing, and Ian too. They were both here all night."

"Oh." She felt weak with relief. "Carla, don't tell them—"

"Of course I won't," Carla said warmly, reaching over to squeeze her hand. "An ordeal such as you've been through is enough to make you suspect everyone."

"But how did they know about the old house, that I might have gone there?"

"It was Byron. He recalled that you had told him of your bad dream and how you saw a painting in Ian's studio of the exact same house. Ian knew immediately where he meant."

Contritely, Andrea remembered how she had thought Byron was unsympathetic, but he had remembered it, and thought it important enough to investigate. A warmth of gratitude overwhelmed her. He *had* been listening to her.

"In any event, Byron and Ian should be coming back shortly since they won't find you there," Carla said.

"We'll have to report this," Randolph told them.

"Yes," Carla agreed. "I'll call the township police now and let them take it from there."

Officer Gordon Heiler arrived almost immediately after Carla's call. Andrea was surprised to see that Frank had come with him. As if in answer to her unspoken question, Gordon told her: "My son attended your party the other evening, and he wanted to come along and offer any support or help he can."

Gordon was a big, overweight man.

Andrea found him both genial and sympathetic. He took her statement carefully, stopping her frequently to question her in detail, then going back over the statement to reread and double-check for accuracy. When he appeared satisfied that he had gotten all the details, he left. Frank remained behind.

Byron and Ian arrived back almost as soon as Gordon left. Both, to Andrea's surprise and delight, enveloped her in warm hugs. In the moment that Byron held her tight, she realized how comfortable she felt in his arms, as if she belonged there.

"I'm so glad you're safe," he murmured, and she could see the relief in his eyes when he released her.

Gordon had taken away the warning letter she had found in her purse, but as the seven of them remained in Carla's kitchen, crowded around the table, it was uppermost in their discussion. "It hardly seems real," Frank remarked. "It's more like a Halloween prank gone wrong."

"It was real enough, as far as I'm concerned," Andrea said with a shudder.

Byron slipped a comforting arm over her shoulders.

"And you don't have a clue in the world as to who did it?" Frank asked.

"Oh, absolutely!" She looked back into Frank's astonished face. "I *know* who did it, almost certainly—it was whoever killed Cheryl. The warning made that clear. Get out and stop snooping, stop trying to solve an old crime. Now all we have to do is find out who that person is."

"Looks like it might have occurred to the murderer that kidnapping you and warning you off was one sure way to reopen the investigation," Byron said. "I'd say the killer or killers are getting pretty desperate and running scared, or they wouldn't have taken that chance."

"Oh, I don't know." Frank shook his head. "Cheryl was nothing but a petty criminal herself. I doubt if whoever did it expected much police time would be wasted on finding someone. . . ."

Andrea glanced at Ian.

"What one lawbreaker does to another," Frank continued, "isn't always that important when the time can be better spent protecting innocent people."

Andrea suddenly remembered Jade and Tony. *What one lawbreaker does to another.* . . . They were at that party Carla had given, and Byron had said at the time there were criminals and suspects present. If not those two, whom would he have been referring to? But Byron seemed to have something going with them, and it was something he didn't intend to tell her.

By late afternoon, Andrea thought her ordeal might as well have been publicized on the nightly news. Somehow the story had spread like wildfire—people dropped by to offer sympathy, to ask curious questions, or even to offer clues, none of which could possibly have been relevant.

As darkness fell, Carla's living room was filled with the same group of people who had attended her party a few evenings previously. "I told you no good would come from flaunting that graven image of the devil on the dinner table," Lydia said sourly as she brought in a tray of refreshments. She stood for a minute, observing them. Her face, Andrea thought, had the wild look of an avenging angel.

"Lydia, really, what *are* you talking about?" Ellen Bentley asked sharply. Lydia only gave her a dark look and left the room.

"She means that little Halloween centerpiece," Carla explained with a humorous smile. "Lydia believes the Jersey Devil literally inhabits our world, and in making the papier-mâché effigy, I've invited doom on all our heads."

Simon looked incredulous. "I've heard that Jersey Devil legend all my life, but I never knew anyone before who actually took it seriously!"

"What were you doing in that old house in the first place?" Antonia asked Andrea. "Weren't you trespassing?"

"Possibly," Andrea admitted. "Yes, I suppose I was. It wasn't posted, however, and the door was open."

"But why did you want to go inside?" Antonia persisted. "What did you expect to find in there? Some clue to that old crime? You *are* still investigating that, aren't you?"

"I never *was* investigating Cheryl's murder, if that's what you're referring to. I came out here to write a series about the Jersey Shore in general. Somehow, possibly because I look like Cheryl, everyone has been determined to link me to her."

"She's right," Randolph said crisply. "She never did have an assignment to look into a murder. She was just here to do a series on the seashore. I'd say it's someone's guilt that has assigned her to the investigation."

"But if you *were* investigating the murder, you wouldn't say so, would you? You wouldn't tell us." Tony looked at her with a knowing smile. "You'd deny it, wouldn't you?"

"I knew all along that's what you were doing," Jade told her. "You never did fool me. I know there's some connection between you and Cheryl!"

Andrea stared at her, aghast. Had it been Tony and Jade last night who had overpowered and drugged her? Surely if it had, they wouldn't be here now, would they? Yet, who else here could it be? And she was convinced that the guilty persons were present in this room.

There was something suspicious about this pair. She listened intently while they talked, trying to discern any nuance in their voices that would give them away or link them to the voices she heard last night. Of course their speech had been disguised. Still, that shriek on the telephone, repeated again when she was kidnapped—couldn't that easily have been Jade? Her voice had the same shrill harshness. . . .

Andrea turned her attention to Bertha and Warren, who had arrived, as before, in their farm pickup truck. While there was something about them that spoke of belonging to a distant decade, surely these people would know nothing of kidnappers who shrieked in the night, of people who committed murder. Their easy rapport with Carla, incongruous as they seemed together, was enough to give her confidence that they had not been the perpetrators.

Frank was solicitous, almost obsequious in his efforts to attend to her, anticipating and getting refreshments before she was ready for them. It was as if he took his father's position as defender of the law a step further, and had appointed himself as her protector. His attention made her nervous. He had just seated himself beside her on the sofa and reached to refill her glass when Antonia came over and sat on her other side.

"Frank and I saw a good movie last night," she informed Andrea. "*Hunter's Quarry.* It's all about this psycho who lives in a cabin in the hills, and he had been stalking the heroine for a long time before she knew about him."

"Antonia," Frank said, "I think that story is a little too *real* to interest Andrea, don't you?"

"Well, I enjoyed the movie," she said sulkily. "I just thought it was interesting that while Andrea was being held hostage in a cabin, we were seeing a movie about the same kind of thing. Odd coincidence, you know, that kind of thing. . . . Anyway, I think it's a good movie and she might even like to see it sometime."

Andrea, astonished by this monologue, observed Antonia. Was she for real? And why did she always seem to be with Frank? And it was Frank who had made that disparaging remark about Antonia being an old maid! There just didn't seem to be a single thing they had in common. Antonia had to be at least fifteen years his senior. Her prim look and proper background clashed utterly with Frank's almost disreputable facade. Their friendship made no sense at all. Was Antonia really so gauche as to be telling her about a stalker and a cabin, or did she have some ulterior motive?

"I think it would be exciting to be kidnapped and kept in a cabin in the pine barrens," Antonia continued, her eyes suddenly bright. "I used to daydream about that when I was growing up. Whatever boy I had a crush on, I'd pretend he took me away to this old abandoned cabin. . . ."

"Excuse me," Andrea said, getting up. She moved off to the kitchen where she found Ian helping Lydia with the refreshments.

"Ian," she said, musing, "I'd like to go back to Leeds Point and look around, but—"

"You're afraid?" He turned and looked at her shrewdly. She nodded. "Would you like me to come with you?"

"Oh, Ian, would you?"

He looked at her for a long moment, as if considering. "I once said I'd never go any nearer to Leeds Point than where I live now," he said. "But having gone there looking for you this morning, I've already broken that vow, haven't I?"

"Then you *will* come with me?"

"What do you hope to find there?"

"I don't know. I really don't. Probably nothing in Leeds Point. But that old house, Ian, I've seen it before. I know I have, long before I ever saw it in your painting. I think I may have lived there once."

He stared at her as if she had taken leave of her senses. "Nobody ever lived there but the Setter tribe."

"But, Ian, I remember the Setters. When I was a child. I can't have memories of a place and people I never saw, can I? And I do . . . memories a long time before Philadelphia."

Chapter Ten

Morning dawned clear and sharp. Frost had painted the early hours white, but now, in the later sunshine, the autumn-blooming chrysanthemums and grass, still green, contrasted brighter than ever against the browns and grays of the season that was rapidly edging toward winter. Yet the sunshine touching over the landscape was a portent of later warmth.

As promised, Ian had called for her early, and they had stopped to have breakfast in a little restaurant in Absecon.

"And you really do think you may be related to the Setters, to Lora, my ex-wife?" Ian stared at her searchingly.

"I'm sure of it. I don't know how, but I remember that house. I *lived* in it once, I know I did. I knew where things were—doors, stairs, rooms. My mother lived there too. I could recall little things about her in connection with the place once I was inside it. And you said yourself that no one other than the Setters lived there during my childhood. . . ."

"It hardly makes sense, though, when you consider who they were, and who you are now. Society Hill bred, Bryn Mawr educated." He shook his head at the contrast that seemed to be beyond his comprehension.

"And there was the fact that my mother would *never* come near this seashore, nor would she allow me to come," Andrea said. "There had to be some secret here in her past that she didn't want me to know. You told me there was a large, extended family living under that one roof. I think she may have been a cousin in the family, and maybe she only visited for short periods. But I *know* we were there."

Ian looked at her doubtfully. "You've been through a bad time in connection with the Setter place. Isn't it possible it just seems magnified, especially in view of what happened to you there?"

Andrea shook her head adamantly. "It's more than that. And, good or bad, I want to know. Wouldn't you?"

"I think maybe not. Sometimes it's better not to pry into the past. Sometimes you discover things you would rather not have known. And if it was anything to your advantage, don't you think your parents would have told you? You may go there and open Pandora's box, you know."

"I was still in my teens when they died. It might have been something I would have been told one day. Ian, haven't you ever wondered why I look so much like Cheryl? When Byron brought the photograph to me, I thought it might well have been my own image."

He considered her thoughtfully, frowning as he buttered his toast. "You look like her, yes. But I never saw as much of her in you as other people seem to. I hate to say this, but there was a hardness in Cheryl that you don't have. You do look like Lora Setter, the way I once saw her, but that could be a coincidence."

She smiled at him and reached across the table to touch his hand. "Whether you agree with me or not, I do appreciate your coming along, Ian. There's no one I'd rather have on this . . . pilgrimage."

He smiled at her and patted her hand back, blue eyes regarding her kindly. "And I'm honored that you feel that way. You're a lovely person, Andrea. If I'd been more fortunate, you might have been my daughter."

Later, breakfast over, and on the road again, Andrea wondered whom they might contact. "Do you suppose any of the Setter family still live around there somewhere?" she asked. "Or were there people who knew them whom we might talk to?"

"I've been thinking of Mavis Harvey. We might visit her."

"Who is she?"

"She was a friend of my former mother-in-law's. A kind woman. If Mavis is still around, I'd rather talk to her than any of the Setters."

"Your mother-in-law. That would have been Lora's mother. What was she like?"

"She was all right. I always thought her ambitions were unrealistic, considering the family she married into. John Setter, her husband, was a poor provider at best, yet she thought Lora should have done better than marry an impoverished sailor, such as I was in those days."

"Maybe they still live around here. Could we talk to them?"

"No. John has been dead for years. He died while I was still married to Lora. And I heard she—Lora's mother—left not long afterward."

In spite of the haunting nature of this trek into the past, Andrea felt her spirits lift unaccountably as they drove. She watched Ian turn the car in the direction of the Setter house without any of the terror she had expected to feel. It was as if the people who had kidnapped her no longer existed, or if they did, they had no more importance than the legend of the Jersey Devil. She felt that something quite startling and wonderful was about to happen to her.

When Ian drew up to the front of the house, he sighed heavily and sat, making no move to get out of the car as he stared out the window. Andrea felt a twinge of remorse that she had subjected this gentle man to what must be a painful memory. "I'm sorry, Ian," she murmured. "I shouldn't have asked you to come here."

"On the contrary, I'm glad you did.

Sometimes it's better if we face things instead of pretending, or half pretending, they never happened. When I was just a kid growing up, I thought Lora Setter was the prettiest girl I ever saw. She had pale brown eyes—huge eyes—and hair like yours. Because we were dirt-poor outcasts and the same age, it was natural, I guess, that we turned to each other for support, to band together against the social structure that rejected us. It was a kind of 'us against them' syndrome in the beginning."

"And later you loved her very much, didn't you?" Andrea whispered, almost able to see the children they had been—their small ghosts still haunting this old Halloween house. Had they once played in this gnarled clump of lilacs, dug in the sand along the shore, and dreamed their separate dreams—Lora's to get what she thought the world owed her, and Ian's to make something better of himself? She felt an ache constrict her throat for what life otherwise might have been for them, and for the daughter Ian had been cheated of knowing.

"No," he said. "It wasn't Lora I loved. I was only in love with who I thought she was. I didn't know her, not at all. She was a dream I'd built up in my mind, but with no more substance than the sea mist. The woman I thought Lora was could never have done the things she did. Sometimes youth does that to us. We want things to be a certain way, and we convince ourselves it is—until reality comes along and slaps us down. Well, come on, if you want to go inside."

He wrapped a large, protective arm around her shoulders as they stepped across the threshold. "I brought a flash-light," he said, fishing in his coat pocket. "It will not only enable us to see where we're going, but if those thugs left behind some clues, maybe it will help us see them."

"It was here," she told him when they had almost finished their tour of the house. "This room—this is where my mother and I stayed when we were here. This is the same wallpaper." She touched the wall, revealing in the flashlight's pale glow a sun-faded pattern of roses growing over a trellis. "It was here I used to wake up in the morning and see these roses. And this window overlooked the widow's walk—what was left of it. It was already rotted then. There's a door that opens on it, and I remember my mother used to keep it bolted because she was afraid I'd step out there and fall through the floor."

A quicksilver, elusive kind of excitement ran through her like electricity. The memory wasn't a bad one, but it wasn't especially good, either. It was just there, just some fact of her early existence. But she had gone away from this place and she had lived her life somewhere else. Why had she been here at all? Ian had no answer, nor did she.

They went back down the dark stairway, Ian shining the light in front of her, and searched among the rooms of the first floor again and again. It was as if the kidnappers had simply never been there, as if the whole episode was just another nightmare. They had left behind no clues at all.

"Well," Ian said at last, "let's go and see if we can find Mavis Harvey. Mavis was the nearest neighbor to the Setters up in that direction." He pointed up the beach. "It's been many years, of course. I don't know that we'll find her at all."

Andrea looked around her as they

came out into the sunshine. The pungent smell of pines was sharply familiar. She had always loved that scent when they went to the house in the Poconos, but she knew that it was here she had experienced it first. The great arm of the ocean that moved in close was a dazzle of brilliance under the sapphire autumn sky. She hoped fervently that Mavis still lived nearby.

Soon they found out that she did. The house, a small, weather-beaten cottage, lay back in a grove of pines. Before they came upon the house, Andrea could see a wreath of smoke that rose straight above the treetops. As they came up the drive, she could see that the blue-gray vapor came from a chimney.

The woman who opened the door leaned heavily on a cane, but she peered at them with alert, dark eyes. When Ian had made her understand who he was, she invited them into her living room. The smoke, Andrea saw, came not from a fireplace as she had thought, but from an ornate stove in the center of the room. Through its glass doors she could see bright coals and blue flames.

The room was sparsely furnished, but

cozy and warm. Mavis fussed greatly over Ian, all but ignoring her. Ian shook his head at her when Andrea tried to interrupt. "Let her talk herself out," he said, when Mavis had hobbled off to the kitchen to make a pot of tea, and "see what else I can find to set a proper snack. Land, I never thought to see you again, Ian Gershner!"

"Stay here. I'll go help her with the tea. She probably has few visitors and wants to make the most of having company. You can question her later."

Mavis turned to Andrea when she came back from the kitchen. "I knew Ian when he was knee-high to a grasshopper," she said. "The dearest little boy. Put away somewhere, I think I have pictures he used to draw and give to me. And to think, he grew up to be a famous man! Here, let me go look for them while you have your tea."

Ian smiled at her while they drank their tea and nibbled cookies, waiting for Mavis to return. "In my urgency to be gone from this place, to stay away from my early defeats," he said, "I'd almost forgotten Mavis. She was one of the people who was kind to me in those early years. I could always count on her for a cookie or a sandwich if I was hungry. I'm glad you brought me here. I'm glad we came back."

We, Andrea thought. *We came back.* Yet, hadn't they both lived here once? And wasn't she, no doubt, some distant cousin of Ian's wife, and therefore also related to Cheryl, his daughter? She was impatient to know what information this frail woman might have that would provide a clue as to why she had been here.

Mavis returned after an interval, bearing an old scrapbook, offering its contents as others might an album of family photographs.

Ian's unmistakable talent was there in his long-ago, childish work. Even in those faraway years, he had already begun to capture some of the mysticism of the sea. The gulls that screamed above the beach were almost audible in their flight. Andrea handled the fragile papers reverently, looking beyond them, seeing the small, lonely boy who had taken that loneliness and translated it into a thing of beauty.

"This one you gave me for Christmas," Mavis said, turning toward the back of the scrapbook and lifting out an oil done on a scrap of canvas. "I gave you a box of paints that year—Christmas Eve, it was—and on Christmas Day, you came back with this, already dry and gift-wrapped. Do you remember?"

"I do now. I'd forgotten. . . . It's a shame, Mavis, but in my bitterness I forgot a lot of things. No man should do that—shut off all the people of his past because of a few bad things that happened. . . ."

"Yes, I always thought it was the way your marriage went that made you stay away. I remember Lora Setter"—she glanced at Andrea—"and how she meant everything to you. Her mother was my friend, but Lora, well, she was a Setter. What more can you say?" She sighed, shifted in her chair, and lifted the teapot, refilling their cups.

"Speaking of the Setters, Mavis, Andrea thinks she remembers visiting them, perhaps for an extended time when she was a child. We were hoping you might have some information that would help her recall her connection with those people."

Mavis paused, still holding the teapot

in her thin, fragile hands. Andrea stared at them, blue-veined, almost transparent in the shaft of sunlight that pushed between the curtains on the window. Later, she knew it was a memory that would remain forever etched in her mind: the sunlight, the warm room, this fragile, gray-haired woman, this huge, gentle giant of a man in his blue sweater.

Mavis stared at the two of them as if they were children who had asked a foolish question. "What do you mean, her connection? *Andrea?* Why, she's your daughter! Yours and Lora's!"

Chapter Eleven

Carla and Jeannie were working outdoors when Ian came roaring up in his aging Jaguar. They looked up from where they were mulching the perennial beds, a little bemused by his uncustomary haste. They watched as he and Andrea got out of the car and came rushing toward them.

"Ian! What is it? Did you find—" Carla asked, only to be interrupted in midsentence.

"Do you know who this is?" Ian demanded, reaching for Andrea's arm. "Do you? Do you know?" His rich, deep voice sang out exultantly.

Andrea, half laughing, half crying, felt herself picked up and swung off her feet, Ian lifting her as easily as if she were still a child.

Carla, still kneeling, weight on her toes, rocked backward, falling awkwardly against the stone wall of the flower bed. "Ian!" she cried, surprised.

Jeannie dropped her pail of mulch, lifting her hand, trowel and all, to brush it across her eyes as if she expected the gesture to clear her vision. Her mouth hung open in astonishment.

"She's mine!" Ian sang out. "She's mine. Mine, mine, mine! My child, my daughter!"

It was some time later, both of them talking and laughing at once, before they were able to convince Carla and Jeannie that they hadn't simply taken leave of their senses.

"But how do you *know?*" Jeannie asked when they had all gone inside. "Just because some woman you don't even remember *thinks* you are doesn't make it so."

"Of course that's what I—we both thought at first," Andrea said, recounting for them the remarkable conversation they had with Mavis Harvey.

"No, you're mistaken," Andrea had said immediately when Mavis had made her stunning statement. "My parents were both from Philadelphia—George and Catilla Maxwell. It's just that I have some memory of being here at the Setters' place with my mother. . . ."

"Lora Gershner was your mother, child. Catilla Setter was *her* mother, and your grandmother."

"You have to be mistaken. You must have some other Catilla confused with my mother. Her name was Maxwell, not Setter."

"Humpf," Mavis said, giving her a long stare. "How many people did you ever know named Catilla?"

"Only one," Andrea said in a small voice. "I thought the name was unique to my mother. She told me her own mother gave her that name because it had come to her in a dream. . . ."

"Same story she told me. It's my body that's crippled, young woman, not my mind! I remember Catilla Vincent Setter as well as I remember anybody. She was my friend for twenty-some-odd years."

"Vincent," Andrea murmured. "That *was* my mother's maiden name. . . ."

"Of course it was. It was *Catilla's* maiden name—she was your grandmother, not your mother."

"And Catilla Vincent Setter was Lora's mother, for sure," Ian said.

"But what was she doing out here, married to a Setter?"

"Catilla Vincent was only seventeen years old when she met John Setter," Mavis said. "She had come out here to the shore for a summer weekend. She was like a lot of other girls at that age. They let their hormones rule their heads. And John Setter was a good-looking boy. Whatever else you might want to say about the Setters, they did have that going for them—good looks. Anyway, Catilla eloped with John and came to live with the Setters in that big old house down there.

"She was only eighteen years old when Lora was born, and she already knew her hasty marriage had been a bad move. But she had a child, a husband, and not much education, and her own family was dead. So she stuck it out." Mavis paused and looked at Ian. "Lora was seventeen when she married you, wasn't she?"

He nodded. "I enlisted in the Navy that same month. I was only eighteen myself."

"And when Lora was eighteen, *you*

were born," she continued, looking at Andrea. "A gray, cold, autumn day—November tenth, it was. I was the midwife who brought you into the world. I remember you had a little star-shape birthmark just below your collarbone. 'Her lucky star,' your grandmother said."

Andrea unconsciously reached up to touch the small mark, shaped like a star, that lay beneath her sweater.

"Lora was not"—Mavis paused, looking at both of them—"what you'd call maternal. I think she had it in the back of her mind that, having her baby at home, she might more easily turn it over to her mother to raise, and more easily forget that she was a mother herself. Lora already had delusions that she might use her good looks to move into entertainment. You weren't more than a week old when she got herself a job as a dancer at one of the sleazy nightclubs in Atlantic City."

Ian shook his head as if pained to be presented with this picture of his early love.

"I guess it's no secret to you that she

soon took up with that Steven Forge, Ian."

He nodded. "But I never knew there was a child. Lora—nobody told me."

"Lora forgot there was one," Mavis told him. "It was Catilla who took care of you, Andrea. She used to say that having you was like getting a second chance—that you were going to grow up different from the Setters, and never be in any way at all like your mother."

"Did you keep in touch with her in later years?" Andrea asked.

"For a while. After some years she stopped writing to me. I guess she just wanted to forget this part of her life had ever happened. I think when John Setter died, it was more a relief to her than a regret. She went back to Philadelphia soon afterward. She took you with her and got a job. That was when she met George Maxwell—he owned the business where she worked, you know. He was a widower with no family and it wasn't long before he married her. Seems they raised you as their daughter, then?"

"But who was Cheryl? She was Lora's daughter, not I!" Andrea said after some minutes of disbelief.

"Yes, Cheryl was her daughter too. But she was born of her marriage to Steven Forge. Born just before he deserted her."

"But what happened to Lora and the other Setters? Don't any of them still live here?"

Mavis shook her head. "I don't know. They've all been gone a long time. As for Lora, well, I always suspected somebody may have killed her. And it was no surprise the way Cheryl went. She was a pretty little thing as a baby. Lora was completely estranged from her mother by that time, and she had no one to take Cheryl, so she farmed her out to those Kendexters most of the time. I guess Cheryl grew up thinking she belonged to them, the way you grew up thinking you were your grandmother's child."

"But according to the police report of Cheryl's death, she was born at the time Lora and Ian were married," Andrea said.

"As I said before, young woman, it's not my mind that's crippled. I remember both births!"

"According to the information Byron had, Cheryl dropped out of school in eighth grade," Ian said. "She would have had to pretend to be older to do the kind of work she did."

"And therefore moved the date of her birth back a few years!" Andrea said.

"Right!"

Only then had they stared at each other with the beginnings of belief.

"And to think," Andrea said now, back at Carla's house, "I'd followed Ian's career, never dreaming—"

"It's unbelievable," Jeannie said, shaking her head in bewilderment.

"Doesn't it make you resent your mother—grandmother, I mean—and George Maxwell because they never told you? Look at all the years you wasted," Carla said sadly.

"Not really. I loved them. They were my parents as far as I was concerned. And no one ever had better. Still, I think I would have been told eventually, if Mom had lived."

"I can't say I hate them for it, either," Ian said. "After all, they loved my daughter and did what they could to give her a good life. I'm sure Catilla did only what she thought was best for Andrea,

Lora being the kind of mother she would have been. And I was away at sea all those years. No. She did the best she knew how. It's Lora I blame, not her mother."

"I can't wait to tell Randolph and Byron!" Andrea said.

"Randy had to go back to Philadelphia. He'll be here this evening in time for dinner," Jeannie explained.

"And Byron is in court today," Carla told her. "He called earlier and left a message for you. He said he'll see you at six o'clock."

"Is Randolph still planning to pursue the investigation as to who murdered Cheryl?" Andrea asked.

"He is. And he'll be more determined than ever, considering your discovery of who she was."

"So am I. I need to know what happened to Lora too. . . ." Andrea broke off with a shudder.

"But it frightens me," Jeannie said. "I'm so scared for both of you. Whoever did this will stop at nothing to prevent your knowing."

"Yes, that's true." Andrea remembered, for the first time in hours, that she already had been kidnapped and warned away. The murderer was still very much at large.

"You could *both* be the next victims," Jeannie said, as if reading her mind.

Chapter Twelve

As Andrea drove along the ridge in northeastern Pennsylvania, she saw that a few lazy snowflakes had begun to fall. She hoped it would be only a flurry, but it was possible to have snow on the ground at this time of year. She hoped to find what she was looking for and to return to Carla's tonight. And a heavy snowfall would hamper her return.

This trip had not been planned at all. It had been almost impossible to sleep last night after the stunning information they had gotten from Mavis. She had awakened several times during the night and reviewed the whole episode. And each time, she wondered what, if anything, her mother—grandmother—might have left behind that would confirm the truth of her birth. She couldn't possibly have intended that she never know. Catilla Maxwell simply wasn't that kind of person.

The memorabilia of their earlier lives was stored in the cabin in the Poconos. All had been removed to this place when the Society Hill house had been sold. She had never sorted through any of it. Actually, after it had been stored, it was some years before she had come back to the cabin.

At the time of her parents' accident, she had been too young to come alone. It wasn't until her college years that she had started coming again, and then it was for weekend trips, driving up with friends. They had often come to ski in winter, but she never had been motivated to sort through the old papers. She hoped the boxes stored in the attic were still intact.

When she had awakened the last time, the night had been edging toward morning. Knowing she wouldn't go back to sleep, she had dressed, left a note in her bedroom for Carla, and slipped quietly out of the house to start this spur-of-the-moment trek.

Used to driving up from Philadelphia on the northeast extension of the Pennsylvania Turnpike, Andrea had become lost twice in the early hours before daylight. The Garden State Parkway had taken her from Somers Point to North Jersey, but she had difficulty after leaving it. She had to cross the state on unfamiliar highways and had taken the wrong route twice.

That was behind her now, however. She had come through the Delaware Water Gap, Stroudsburg, and was now driving the high ridge that shortly would take her to her destination.

In the gray dawn, she had noticed numerous cars parked off the highway. It dawned on her that it was hunting season. The Pennsylvania woods were full of hunters during this time of year. They came from everywhere to harry the wild creatures. She recalled the ongoing battle her family had waged to keep hunters off the property. Although her parents had posted many notices against hunting, it seldom deterred persistent poachers. She hoped to get through the day and leave without the necessity of having a confrontation with any of them.

"Cabin" was not an exact description of the Poconos property. "We might as well stay in Philadelphia as buy into one of those resort developments," she remembered her parents deciding when they had first begun to look for the place. Andrea had been about nine years old then, and became utterly fascinated with the place they had bought—a small, isolated farm nestled in a clump of white birches on the very top of a ridge.

The small white house had wide front and back porches that sheltered out summer storms, where she used to play. There was a barn to the rear, which, functional in its previous years, was now unused but picturesque. She, too, was glad they had bought this old farm instead of cabins clustered close and of similar design.

Deciding to buy breakfast instead of making her own, she pulled off at a roadside diner. The place was already filled up with hunters, crowding all the tables with their Day-Glo orange clothing. She found a vacant stool at the counter and seated herself. "Hi, Bob!" She smiled at the big, gray-haired, white-aproned man who was working quickly behind the counter.

He paused, coffeepot raised to refill customers' cups. "Well, well, hello there, Andy!" he said, using her childhood nickname. A delighted grin spread across his face. "Didn't expect to see you in this crowd. Why didn't you let us know? We'd have turned the heat up and had the house warm for you."

"Sudden decision," she told him. "Nobody even knows I'm up here. Think it's going to snow?"

"Probably not much. Weather report last night said we might get an inch here in the higher elevations. You never can tell, though. Weatherman has been known to miss it. Staying a few days?"

"No. I just came to pick up something. I'm going back as soon as I find it. How about making one of your great pancake breakfasts for me—or are you too busy now? Don't go to any extra trouble if that's not on your menu."

"Anything you want is on the menu, Andy. You know that. Pancakes, it is!"

Bob Yakowski and his wife, Sandra, were the nearest neighbors, living on the farm next to hers out on the highway. They had been good friends all the years her family had come here, and it was they who had looked after the house when it was empty. Her place was just around the next curve in the highway, and she ate her breakfast quickly, watching the snowflakes coming down outside. If she hurried, maybe she would find what she was looking for and be on her way back to New Jersey shortly.

"Tell Sandra hello for me," she said to Bob as she paid her bill. "If I had more time, I'd drive up to see her."

"We'll look for you next time. Latchkey is always out for you. You know that."

Once she had turned into her own driveway, she paused, holding her foot lightly on the brake. She had never been able to take this view for granted. It was so much a part of her early years and the many childhood summers spent here. She had missed it acutely all the time it had, of necessity, been vacant. And it was now that she knew beyond a doubt that, whatever Catilla Maxwell's motivations had been in keeping her origins secret, they had been right for her.

The house sat well back from the highway and up a long, winding lane. White birches clumped on either side of the drive, their graceful, white trunks a sharp contrast to the darker bark of other trees. It was a setting straight out of a storybook. Even the house, although quite old, and of no particular architectural design, might well have been the model for illustrating some fey fairy tale. It sat close to the land, hugging the higher rise of hill, its chimneys tall above the sloped lines of roof.

She was grateful for the Yakowskis. If they had not been willing to keep an eye on the place, she would have had to sell it years ago. She eased her foot off the brake and drove up to the front of the house. The snow was coming down faster now, coating the fallen leaves with a dry, white powder.

Inside, she turned the thermostat high. If it continued to snow, she might have to spend the night rather than risk driving back to the shore. Unfortunately, there was no telephone in the house to call Carla, but Bob's diner was only a short drive. She hurried on through the rooms, making a quick check to see that everything was in order. She had learned the importance of this when she was quite young, and the habit held, all these years later. Once, they had arrived to find a black bear had managed to break in, and the beast was sleeping in the kitchen, provisions strewn around him. Now, satisfied that there were no signs of trespassers, human or beast, Andrea hurried up to the attic.

Her attic venture into the past required more time than she expected. It took hours of sorting through boxes before she found it. The story was all there, in a baby book designated simply as *Andrea.* Here was the confirmation of all Mavis had told her.

There, among the usual things doting parents wrote about their children, Catilla had added a journal of her own thoughts and feelings. Here she had poured out her love, her misgivings, and her determination that given this second chance, Andrea Gershner would be different from the Setters, and from Lora, her mother. For this child, life would be as good as she, Catilla, could make it.

There was the birth certificate naming her parents, Lora Setter and Ian Gershner. The last entry Catilla made in the journal had been dated when Andrea was fifteen years old.

I don't know how to undo what has been done, how to tell you without possibly hurting you. But the truth of your birth was kept from you out of love, not to deprive you of your parents. My daughter, Lora, sad to say, simply didn't care. I have an ever-increasing guilt about Ian. Someday soon I suppose you will have to know.

I grieve for George as much as for myself if we lose you. George has never been told that you are my granddaughter. He loved you as his own from the very beginning. I don't need to tell you that! Someday soon, I will simply hand you this book, and after you've read it, hope you will forgive me and remain with us.

Andrea was crying, weeping aloud when she read this final entry. Shortly after it had been written, George and Catilla had been killed. It was only now that she had seen what Catilla had written, knowing she had her permission and her blessing, that she could finally think of her as "Grandmother" and know that she belonged to Ian.

Finally, emotionally spent, Andrea went back downstairs. The house was toasty warm by now. Outside the window the snow continued to fall. She decided Bob was right—the weather forecasters didn't always predict accurately. The ground was white now, a trackless carpet spread across the mountain.

On second look, it wasn't all that trackless. Tire prints in the snow led up to her house and out beyond toward the barn! Hunters! Momentarily furious that they had chosen to disobey the NO HUNTING signs posted where her driveway began, she decided she would go out, get the license number of the car, and drive to Bob's to call the police.

But when she went out on the back porch, she saw that no car was parked by the barn or anywhere in sight. The trespassers had, no doubt, seen that the house was occupied and had gone to poach elsewhere.

When she went back into the house, drowsiness soon overcame her. The warmth inside, the silent snow outside, the isolation, and most of all, her night of missed sleep, caught up with her. Whether she went back today or not, a nap was what she needed now.

Andrea didn't know how long she had been asleep when the dream began. It was a stealthy sound at first, as if a door had been pushed open somewhere and a sharp breath of cold air had come inside, invading the warm room. Whispers went through the house. A floorboard creaked.

After a while, her dream got mixed up with the Setters' empty house where she had returned in sleep, where the Jersey Devil rode the moon, and where she had gone later and found the secret of her past.

Then the Setters' door had creaked open to admit Antonia and Frank. "We could do it here while she's asleep," Frank said. "Be easier."

"No, stupid!" Antonia had almost shouted. "There would be blood all over everything!"

Then Andrea opened her eyes. It wasn't a dream at all. She was staring into their faces: Frank's sneering, Antonia's cold and determined. It was Antonia who held the gun. An evil, snub-nosed revolver was aimed directly at her!

Chapter Thirteen

The passage of time was interminable. Each minute seemed an hour; each hour, a day. Andrea knew with a fatalistic certainty that she was soon to die. She didn't doubt that for one second.

"We warned you once," Antonia told her. "You had your chance to go back to Philadelphia and mind your own business. If you had, this wouldn't have been necessary."

"Then it was you and Frank who followed me to that old house. . . ."

Antonia nodded. "We weren't going to hurt you. We only wanted to scare you, so you'd leave us alone."

"But I don't understand. I wasn't bothering you. I wasn't even interested in you—or Frank."

"You would have been. You soon would have been sent out to investigate Cheryl's death."

If only she could keep them talking,

she might at least buy more time. Andrea pretended ignorance, asking what she already knew, that it was Antonia and Frank who had killed Cheryl. *Too close to the law for the law to investigate.* Lydia's words echoed once again in her mind. Too close to the political power structure too, she realized now that she knew Antonia was involved. Hadn't someone said that Simon Bentley ruled the political scene out there?

"You don't mean to say it was you two who killed my half-sister, do you?" Andrea asked innocently, hoping to put as much disbelief as possible into her voice.

"*I* didn't," Frank said. "It was Antonia." He looked at his accomplice with contempt. "If she'd ever had what it takes to hold on to a man, Cheryl might still be alive."

Antonia turned the gun on him with a look of hate. For a brief, hopeful second, Andrea thought they might simply forget about her and carry on their own feud. She had never figured them for friends in the beginning, and it was obvious now they weren't. They were simply locked together in a common secret—a secret that involved murder and kidnapping.

But Antonia, mindful of the danger her divided attention put her in, turned on Andrea again with the gun.

"Your half-sister," she spat out. "I *knew* there was some blood connection! Cheryl deserved to die. She was nothing but a dirty little tramp."

"But prettier than you," Frank said, as if unable to resist the dig at Antonia.

"She was *not!*" Antonia's shriek of denial was pathetic, and Andrea clearly detected in her voice the unearthly shriek she had heard twice before.

"She took your man away, didn't she?"

"No!" Antonia shrieked again. "No! No! She didn't care about Brent Reid. She was only using him. He would have come back to me when he found her out!"

"But he didn't, did he?" Frank yelled back at her. "You killed Cheryl to get her out of your way, and Brent still wasn't interested in you. Stupid old maid, whatever made you think he was? You were nothing more than a joke to him. He knew all about your hanging around the back of the gravel pit, taking pictures, blackmailing people."

Antonia's face crumpled. She had the look of a small child about to cry. "It's not true," she whispered. "Brent would have come back—I know he would have. He *will* someday. You wait and see."

In spite of her own position, Andrea felt a thrust of pity for this child-woman. For that, she realized, was all she was. There was mania in her eyes, and her face, regardless of the age lines, was one of a five-year-old who had lost something important to her small world. And she had lashed out with lethal force at the person whom she had seen as being responsible for taking it away from her. Antonia Bentley was clearly not sane.

"But why did you get involved?" Andrea asked Frank. Possibly she could appeal to something saner in him.

"Frank didn't have any choice," Antonia said, pride touching her voice. "When Cheryl was dead and I couldn't move her body, I called him."

"But why did you respond?" Andrea asked again. "Why did you put yourself in a position to be an accomplice to murder?"

"Blackmail, what else?" Frank said with a bitter twist to his mouth. "You don't think I'd choose a loon like this for a *friend,* do you?"

"He had no choice," Antonia told her impatiently. "I knew too much about Frank. And I know even more about his dad. I saw Gordon kill Lora Forge."

"Gordon Heiler. . . . The *policeman* killed my mother?" Andrea stared at the two of them. Surely none of this was happening. It was a dream. Just another strange dream and she would awaken. . . . "But that makes no sense at all! Why would he kill Lora?"

"Because he wanted to break off with her and she wouldn't let him," Antonia said. "They'd been having an affair, and he'd covered up for her when she was involved in a burglary. When he tried to break up with her, she threatened to go to his wife—and to the town. He'd lose his family and his job. They had a big fight. He knocked her down, and she hit her head. He took her body out in a boat and dumped it in the ocean."

"How do you know all this?" Andrea demanded. "Why would he have allowed you to be a witness?"

"Oh, he didn't know anything about it at the time," Antonia said airily. "The back part of the gravel pit, where all the more interesting things happen, adjoins our estate. It's easy to see through that high hedge of shrubbery and to watch what's going on. Some of the things I've seen and heard. . . ." A dreamy expression came over her face.

"But doesn't that kind of information put *your* life in danger? If he killed Lora, why wouldn't he also kill you to keep you quiet?"

"You don't think I'm stupid, do you? I never go down there to watch people without my camera. And I print the pictures in my own darkroom. I got pictures of Gordon and Lora fighting, pictures of him hitting her. I followed him to the ocean and got pictures of him taking her body out in the boat. Then I sent him prints along with the message that if anything ever happens to me, I've left instructions as to where to find the negatives. If that happened, it would be all over for him. No. It's worth everything in the world to Gordon to keep me alive and healthy!"

Dazed, Andrea shook her head. It was

a dream. It *had* to be! And yet, the reality of it was with her. She, too, would soon be another victim.

"We'll keep her here until it's almost dark," Antonia told Frank. "Then we'll take her back into the woods to shoot her. It's hunting season. Who's to notice one more gunshot with all the others around? And when her body is found, *if* it ever is, what's one more hunting accident?"

"But . . . how did you find me?" Andrea asked. "Surely you didn't follow me. I left New Jersey at four o'clock this morning!"

Frank shook his head. "Carla called the police when she found you were missing. My dad went out, and while he was there, they found the note you left in your room."

"And we knew this was our best chance," Antonia added.

Ages later, Andrea wondered why she had heard no sound. Her first inkling that they were not alone had been the look of sheer terror that had crossed Antonia's face, which had gone deadly white. Suddenly she let the gun fall, her mouth dropping open as she looked beyond Andrea.

It was only when Andrea turned that she saw them. The room was filling up, it seemed, in that electrifying second, with all the people in the world about whom she cared most. Ian, Carla, Byron, Jeannie, Randolph—even Bob Yakowski—they were all there. There was only one stranger, a state policeman taking her captors into custody.

Byron reached out to draw her into his arms. "Are you all right, Andrea?"

"I am now," she said, snuggling close, wanting to stay in his arms forever.

Everyone started speaking at once.

"But, Andrea, what on earth? What made you leave in the middle of the night and come here without telling anybody?"

"Antonia and Frank! Who would have ever dreamed. . . ."

"I wanted to kill them both when I first saw. . . ."

"But what were you *doing* here?"

"Okay, now. That's enough! Let's not all talk at once, or we'll *never* make sense of this," Jeannie said, clapping her hands for silence. "One question at a time."

"Me first," Andrea said weakly. "Considering I just missed being murdered, tell me how you knew. How did you find me?"

"Okay, Bob," Jeannie said, still refereeing, "you tell her."

"I thought there was something funny about that yahoo in the dark glasses the minute he came in the diner asking if I knew where you lived," Bob said. "When I questioned him, he said they'd come out here to meet you and go hunting. Then when he was gone, I got to thinking. *Andy,* I said to myself, *hunting? Why, Andy would just as soon let a band of cutthroats and murderers on her property as invite hunters!* And then I remembered that you'd told me nobody knew you were even here and you'd just come to pick something up. I'd just called the police when this carload of people came looking for you. We followed the policeman out here."

"We were so worried when we got up and you weren't there," Carla said. "I called Ian and Byron, and when we found your note, we were even more worried. The thought of your going off into the woods by yourself when you'd just been kidnapped. . . ."

"We were almost certain that whoever did this would be tracing your movements, and that they would surely follow you," Byron said, still holding Andrea tightly.

"So now tell us, why *did* you come up here?" Jeannie asked.

"I wanted to know if my grandmother had left behind any information that would confirm what Mavis told us yesterday. It wasn't that I didn't believe Mavis—it was just, well, I guess I wanted my grandmother's permission to go on and be who I really am."

"And did you find it?" Ian asked.

Andrea nodded and moved over to wrap her arms around her father. "She told me in a journal she kept. Someday, I'll let you read it."

"Well, I guess I'd better be getting back to the diner," Bob said, only to have the entire group converge on him at once, shaking his hand, clapping him on the back, and in Andrea's case, giving him a firm hug.

"I never did introduce you," she said to the others. "Bob Yakowski is one of my dear friends. He and his wife, Sandra, go back a long way—all the way back to my childhood."

"We watched her grow up," Bob told them. "And there's no way I wouldn't have investigated a story like that guy tried to pull on me!"

"Speaking of diners," Andrea said when Bob had gone, "how about we make some dinner? I'm starving!"

"Maybe we could get something on the way," Randolph suggested, looking out the window. "That snow is really coming down, and we ought to be going."

"Oh, must we?" Andrea asked. "Why can't we all stay here? There's lots of room, plenty for everybody, and I . . . I really want to stay here and feel safe, with all of you, for a while." She looked pleadingly into each of their faces, and especially at Byron. She wanted him to know this house and understand its importance to her.

"Sounds good to me," he said, squeezing her hand.

"Sounds even better to me," Ian agreed. "Beautiful country up here! It's the kind of place that could turn an old sea dog like me into a landlubber."

"I'm glad you like it," Andrea told him. "Because you *are* going to be spending a lot of time here in the future!"

"I love this kitchen!" Carla exclaimed when she, Jeannie, and Andrea had gone to look for the makings of dinner while the men went searching for firewood.

"It was completely renovated along with the rest of the house about ten years ago, just before the accident. My . . . grandparents decided that we spent so much time up here, it should be made as comfortable as possible."

"You certainly keep a supply of food on hand—look at all these tins, jars, boxes!" Carla exclaimed.

"We learned to do that years ago. Sometimes you can come up here in winter and be snowbound for days."

"All *right!*" Jeannie said enthusiastically. "I can make a great dinner from this without having to send out for anything!"

"Jeannie, as you may have observed," Andrea said, turning to Carla with a smile, "is a born cook. When we were still in school, I sometimes used to think she came up here with me only to be turned loose in this kitchen."

"Don't knock it until you taste it." Jeannie, collecting ingredients, grinned at them. "I'm going to cook us a meal fit for—for all the things we're going to celebrate!"

The men returned, shaking off snow, exhaling frosty breaths, and bearing firewood. "We found your wood supply," Ian said. "I always knew any daughter of mine would have a passion for roaring fires on winter nights."

"And storms in summer," Andrea told him affectionately. "And coral sunrises streaking the morning sky. . . . I always knew I got my affinity for beauty from somebody. There had to be an artist somewhere in my background."

Much later, when the clock had edged toward midnight, and Ian's fire was a dying glow, Andrea stirred from her dreamy mood and looked at the others. "I hate to bring up unpleasant things after such a lovely evening, but this business about Antonia is so strange. Did anyone ever suspect she might have had something to do with Cheryl's death?"

"Actually, yes, in a way," Byron said. "There were two or three people in the prosecutor's office who were willing to bet that Antonia knew more than she was telling. The Bentley estate being the only occupied house anywhere near the gravel pit, naturally the investigation involved asking what, if anything, they may have seen or heard."

"And what kind of response did they get?" Randolph asked.

"The Bentleys weren't home, or so they said. Only Antonia had been in that weekend. Antonia, however, apparently acted, well, a little bizarre during questioning. . . ."

"She certainly *is* bizarre," Jeannie said with a shudder. "Did you hear her? That unearthly screaming when the policeman led her away? 'Mommy! Daddy! I want my Mommy. . . .' Why, you could hardly believe it was a grown woman."

"In many ways, she's not," Carla said. "Of course I've known the Bentleys only since I moved out to the shore, but Antonia. . . . I don't know, it always seemed to me she was simply someone who had never learned to live, except vicariously, through watching other people."

"But if she was a suspect, why was nothing ever done?" Andrea asked.

"It wouldn't have been popular for the people who suspected her to have pursued it," Byron said. He made a wry grimace. "The guys who suspected owed their very jobs to the patronage of Simon Bentley."

"So what will happen now? Nothing, because someone owes Bentley a favor?"

"Oh, no. This is a whole different ball game. It wouldn't have been smart to investigate with no real evidence. But she's been caught now. There's nothing she can do but confess."

"And that policeman. To think I called him into my home asking for help," Carla said. "If you can't trust the police, who can you trust?"

"Hey, just because a man has taken an oath to uphold the law doesn't always mean he will," Byron said. "You'll often find bad guys where you least expect. But you don't judge the whole lot by the one bad apple."

"So what will happen now?"

"My best guess is that Antonia will be

found not guilty by reason of insanity and sent away somewhere," Byron said. "Frank, I would guess, will get a short sentence in prison, and Gordon Heiler, well, they may throw the book at him. We'll have to wait and see, of course. You never can predict with any certainty what a jury will decide."

Andrea shuddered. "I'm sorry I brought all that up at this hour. It's been such a nice night, otherwise. Let's all talk about something else, or we'll have nightmares."

Carla reached over and touched Ian's arm. "Tell them our news, and we'll end on a happy note before bedtime."

Andrea turned swiftly to look at her father and Carla seated close together on the sofa. The glow from the dying fire touched their faces. She thought with wonder how very young and very happy they both looked at this minute, when Ian spoke. "Carla and I are going to be married," he said simply.

Ian's announcement brought the group to their feet, all talking at once.

"That's wonderful!"

"Congratulations, Ian and Carla!"

"Isn't that the best news ever? Now

we'll be relatives, Andrea, not just former college roommates!"

"It couldn't happen to two nicer people!"

"We'll have to do a piece in *Kaleidoscope* on this—with your permission, of course."

"When will the wedding be?"

Carla and Ian, laughing and receiving congratulations, suddenly became aware that only Andrea had not said a word. "Oh, my dear!" Carla said, getting up and going over to her. "Is it too soon? Is this making you feel like you've found a father, only to lose him? I didn't mean—"

"Oh, Carla, no. This was something I wanted, for both of you. I'm so happy—it was just such a magic moment. To think! A day that was so horrible earlier could end so wonderfully!"

Chapter Fourteen

The sea stretched out glassy and green toward the far horizon. Even now, two months later, Andrea was still amazed by the mercurial moods that settled over this seemingly endless expanse of sky and water. Today, at the end of December, she felt she could look out over the water and see almost into eternity. Sometimes the rains came, the mists rolled in, and the horizon would be almost within arm's reach when the waves rolled high, storm-tossed and crashing. Other days the sea spread out like a gray pavement, broken here and there in heaving, white-capped waves, or it would flatten out, blue and serene, appearing to be only an extension of the sapphire sky.

"What are you thinking?" Byron, edging closer behind her, wrapped his arms around her, pulling her close. They were seated on a tuft of dry dune grass. "You looked so lost and far away."

"I'm not," she assured him, leaning her head back and resting her cheek against his. "I was only thinking how well I understand my father's fascination with the sea. It's like a magnet. I think I want to live here forever."

"I'm glad," he said, moving a hand up to cup her chin and brushing his lips across her hair. "That means *I* can stay here. I was afraid for a while there that you were going back to Philadelphia and I would have to be a city lawyer again, maybe for the rest of my life."

"Would you have? Followed me, I mean, and given up your career here?"

He stood up, pulling her to her feet. "Look at me and ask that! Where you go, I go. My work will always be secondary to what I feel for you."

Andrea squeezed his hand as they started walking off down the deserted beach. The moment was too emotional for any other response.

In spite of her early traumatic experiences, these months had been a lovely interlude. Now that Frank, Gordon, and Antonia were incarcerated and awaiting trial, the sense of danger was no longer there. It had been a time to get acquainted with her father, to develop friendships here at the shore, to continue writing her column. But most of all, it had been a time to fall in love.

She and Byron had been together almost always during the past weeks. Immediately after that frightening experience in the Poconos, she had learned the attraction that she felt for him had been a mutual one. After Antonia and Frank were arrested, he had told her, "All I could think of when we came in and I saw Antonia holding the gun on you, was that I'd waited all my life for you, and you were about to be snatched away from me before we'd had time to live our lives together. I'm surprised the rage I felt toward that pair didn't turn them both to cinders."

"And I thought for a while there weren't going to be any days of my life left," Andrea answered. "You can't know what it was like for me when you burst through that door like an army of avenging angels!"

She supposed all women thought their courtships were unique and special, but she *knew* hers had been. Byron had never seemed at a loss to find things to do.

There was the magic and glitter of city nights—Broadway plays, the Philharmonic, nightclubs—they were all within easy reach. There were the times of shared companionship at Ian's or Carla's fireside, weekends when the four of them returned to the Poconos to tramp through frost-crisp woodland and perform homey chores on the old farm. And there were the quiet times such as this, when they walked the deserted beaches and listened to the lonely, eternal songs of the sea.

They had talked endlessly about anything and everything, including Byron's work. When she told him of her confusion at seeing him talking in the restaurant with Tony and Jade, he explained that Tony was a client, and they had been discussing his case.

They had known from the beginning that their feelings for each other were permanent, but it had been last week, when she had gone to West Virginia with Byron to visit his family for Christmas, that he had given her the ring. She touched her finger now, to feel the ring's solidity through her glove, seeing in her mind the beauty of the blue-white fire.

"Don't you think we'd better start back?" Byron asked, turning her around toward the direction of Ian's house. He checked his watch. "Randolph and Jeannie should be along soon, and we can't be late for your dad's wedding!"

They came out through the pines to the back of the house to find the others had already arrived. Ian and Carla were to be married tonight, New Year's Eve. They wanted to start their new life with the new year, they decided, and it was to be a small, quiet wedding held in Ian's living room in the house by the sea.

They came inside to find that along with Randolph and Jeannie there was a photographer from *Kaleidoscope,* who was already busy setting up in preparation for shooting pictures to be used in the publication.

"This is going to be a real scoop for us," Randolph said. "I can't believe how we've taken off in the last two months. That kind of quick success quite astonishes me."

"A publication that solved two murders and assorted other crimes while still a start-up *has* to get a lot of notice,"

Byron told him. "I hear you're up for awards."

"My daughter is getting a lot of attention with that column too," Ian said proudly. "I'm not surprised that she's going into syndication!"

"*Our* daughter," Carla corrected him firmly. "And it will be wonderful to have one who doesn't live half the world away! Have you given any more thought to whether you will live here or in Philadelphia?"

"Here," Andrea said. "We just decided."

"We also decided to shorten our engagement," Byron said. "We'll be married next month, instead of waiting until June."

"Have you started house hunting yet?" Jeannie asked.

"Not yet, but soon, after we get Carla and Ian off on their honeymoon," Andrea said. "I'm going to stay here while they're gone, and that will give us time to look around."

"Why did you decide all of a sudden that this is where you'll live?" Jeannie asked.

Andrea turned and smiled at Carla.

"Do you remember telling me about an old adage that said if you come to the shore and get sand in your shoes, you may stay on?"

"Forever," Ian said, cutting in solemnly. "Get sand in your shoes, and you'll stay forever!"

Andrea laughed and hugged them both. "And so I came, and I got sand in my shoes."